The Love Song of Maya K

The Love Song of Maya K

and other stories

SHUMA RAHA

NIYOGI
BOOKS

Published by
NIYOGI BOOKS
Block D, Building No. 77,
Okhla Industrial Area, Phase-I,
New Delhi-110 020, INDIA
Tel: 91-11-26816301, 26818960
Email: niyogibooks@gmail.com
Website: www.niyogibooksindia.com

Editor: Mohua Mitra
Cover design: PealiDezine
Layout: Shashi Bhushan Prasad

ISBN: 978-93-86906-39-7
Publication: 2018

Printed at: Niyogi Offset Pvt. Ltd., New Delhi, India

To My Mother

Contents

Smell the Coffee Beans, Please

Sandhya spritzed some eau de parfum on a strip of paper, gave it a wave or two and handed it to the woman. "It's very woody, very refreshing," she said, summoning her most ingratiating smile.

The woman was tall and condescending. She had rigid white hair and diamonds on diverse parts of her dry old body. She held the perfumed strip with her bejewelled, claw-like fingers and sniffed at it dubiously. But Sandhya was ready for her. Before she could voice her dislike, Sandhya offered her another one. "Or try this, Ma'am," she said brightly. "This is a light floral. Do you want it for day wear or evening wear?"

Sandhya was good at her job. She had been working as a sales girl at this perfume counter for over a year. Though she stuck pretty much to the same sales routine that they had all been schooled in, she managed to sell more than any of her colleagues at the other perfume counters in the department store. It made them jealous of her, of course. They sneered at her and called her 'proud'. "Sandhya," they hissed through pursed lips and narrowed eyes, "She's proud!" And they made it sound as if it were the dirtiest word in the world.

In truth, Sandhya was proud. She knew she had a way with customers. She could draw them in with her soft, lilting voice and keep them tempted and ensnared in the fragrances in her armoury. Even casual store-strollers often ended up making an impulse buy if they came under her gentle spell. When she uttered words like "woody" or "citrus" or "spicy", they did not sound unthinking and mechanical, as they did when her colleagues pronounced them. With her, the jargon took on an exquisite meaning and became redolent of a sense of wonder and awe. It was almost as if she were sharing a secret with visitors to her boudoir, unveiling the essence of some precious, closely guarded thing. It was hard not to be affected by her patter. Only, it didn't seem like patter at all, but like a journey into the heart and soul and purpose of the array of fragrances of which she was mistress.

She loved the work. Not just the work–she loved the department store and the glittering shopping mall in which it was housed. When she stepped into the store, made her way to the staff changing room, and took off her everyday clothes, she felt liberated and transformed. Dressed in her uniform of white shirt, black trousers and black jacket, with her hair pulled away from her face and packed into the tight whorl of a bun, she took her place at the perfume counter with the grace of a young queen about to hold court. Myriad perfumes rose up to greet her as she set out the vials of testers on the counter. The air-conditioning lay like balm upon her yearning skin, and her mind, which drifted into a kind of torpor when she was at home, began to glow and hum again. To Sandhya the store was a magic palace, a continually marvellous fairground full of fine and sumptuous things. And each day she thrilled anew to the clothes and the lingerie, the bags and the shoes, the make-up and the watches, and gloried in them as though they were her own.

She lived with her parents and two younger siblings in a one-roomed flat in Kolkata's Kalighat. She had grown up amidst the high religious squalor of the Kali temple's precincts. She had gone to school sidestepping the daily surge of raucous devotees intent on extracting benediction from a fearsome deity. She had picked her way through the mounds of rotting garlands and flowers, the dissipated *jaba* and the putrid *rajanigandha*, the waste and the swill strewn with paper boxes oily with the remnants of sweets gone rancid, and diaphanous plastic bags that drifted like poisonous spores. She had negotiated the pie dogs that sniffed at them and the beggars who sifted through them, and had come back home, not with relief, but with equal revulsion.

Sandhya regarded her home as a prison cell into which she had been thrown by some horrid mistake. The small room, where five people sweated their discontent, was detestable to her. Her nitpicking father, her sickly mother with the worry lines on her forehead, and her loud, quarrelsome siblings—were they really her family, she had begun to wonder as she was growing up. Or was she a changeling who belonged somewhere else? Lying on the floor on a thin *chatai* with her younger brother and sister, Sandhya had dreamed dreams of herself in another time, another place, where she would recline on a creamy satin bed, eating fat purple grapes and playing with her jewels. She would have money aplenty, of course, and heaps of romances too, until one day she would take her pick from a string of rich and handsome suitors.

She had dropped out of college because she was never any good at studies. Besides, her father wanted her to start earning so she could contribute to the household expenses. So she jobbed as a sales girl in a couple of shops in her locality. They were small, rundown establishments, where tired people in shabby clothes came and bargained querulously over cheap synthetic sarees and frocks trimmed with artificial *zari*. And Sandhya, who looked upon anything cheap with a simple, intense hatred, found them intolerable. She felt she couldn't take one more day of the soul-crushing drabness into which she had been flung. When she was a teenager she had wanted to be a film star. But she knew she didn't have the looks for it. She looked pleasant, but she wasn't pretty. Still, she had wanted to run away. Just land up some place and see where fate took her. And then, she got the job at the department store.

She had felt at home from the moment she joined the store. This house of lights, this floor upon floor of unimaginable treasures, this is where she belonged, she had thought happily. And the people! Those pampered, shiny folk with their soft hands and languid faces! The bizarrely fortunate who sauntered in and splashed their cash on a thousand splendid things! She felt she knew them and understood what made them tick. Perhaps that was the secret of her success at the perfume counter. Offering, coaxing, laying them all out for the customers, she felt involved and committed. She participated in their confusion and dilemma (should it be this, or that? Spicy or citrus?) and in the end, shared their joy of possessing something extravagant and evanescent.

And so she persevered with the old lady of the diamonds. "This one, Ma'am? Or try this–this one's really good for summer… just a hint of spiciness. You want to try this again? Sure, Ma'am. Smell the coffee beans, please. Yes, now tell me, isn't that better? I knew you'd like it. I think I have understood exactly what you're looking for."

The woman had large nostrils and she inhaled each perfume-sprayed strip offered to her with such ferocity that one end of it flew up to her nose every time. Unembarrassed, and after many tries and retries, and many noisy inhalations from the pot of coffee beans to cleanse her befuddled olfactory nerves, she finally narrowed her selection to three fragrances. Then suddenly sick of the bother of having to take a decision, she settled for an old favourite that she had worn many times before.

"Excellent choice," Sandhya said with such fervent approval that the woman beamed at her at last.

When she left Sandhya gave a small sigh of contentment and straightened her jacket. Her English was really getting so much better! She could swear that she had carried on the conversation just right. She spoke Hindi correctly and fluently, thanks to the hours of watching Hindi TV serials. And Bengali was, of course, her mother tongue (which, it had to be said, she liked less and less and didn't speak unless she absolutely had to). The vernacular did for most people. But with some customers you just had to speak in English. This woman had seemed like one of them. She had been tiresome, but she certainly had class. And she wore so many diamonds! In the end, she had smiled as though she had really liked her.

Right then Sandhya could have started a story in her head about the old lady of the diamonds who becomes a sort of fairy godmother, swooping into their one-roomed tenement flat in Kalighat and whisking her away. She would adopt her perhaps and Sandhya would go to live in her great house that had a grand wooden staircase and brilliant crystal chandeliers all over. It was an appealing storyline, but Sandhya was busy with numerous other stories to bother dwelling on a fairy godmother scenario. Some of these stories had become frayed around the edges, and some bored her now. Still, there were at least a half a dozen more she was carting around in her head that needed her attention.

The stories were nearly always sparked by a male visitor at her perfume counter. She treated him with the same friendly deference that she deployed in the case of everyone else–smiling and indefatigable in her effort to lead him to the perfect fragrance. However, a stray look or smile on his part, perhaps to acknowledge her enthusiasm or her easy sales talk, was enough to launch the story. In its essence, the story was simple enough. It was about how the man fell in love with her. But Sandhya had too much imagination and inventiveness to make the narratives as straightforward as that. So she fleshed them out–slowly, lovingly. She wove them hour by hour, adding piece upon set piece, changing and improvising, and taking them through numerous twists and turns. Waiting at the bus stop, or during a lull at the perfume counter, washing her clothes in the morning before the water ran out, or when her family was finally asleep at night, Sandhya went tiptoeing back to the multitude of passion plays unfolding and rearing inside her brain. They all wanted her! Those rich, privileged men desired her! And she–coy, resisting, audacious, demanding, now timid, now valiant, now a smouldering sex goddess–lived innumerable fantastical tales. She fed them and fed off them, and felt herself grow beautiful and irresistible like some mythical siren who plays with the hearts of a flotilla of bewitched men.

It was not as if she had never had a romance. There were neighbourhood boys who had made overtures. She had gone to see Hindi movies with them, only to be thrashed by her father when he came to know of it. One love affair had progressed to a fervid exchange of notes and furtive conversations snatched on the way to college. However, it fizzled out after a few months because the boy found a job in Pune and went away. He never contacted her again.

Then there was Abhishek, the guy at the watch counter of the department store who, the other girls said, was definitely sweet on her.

Abhishek was young, about her age, and he had a friendly face and merry, intelligent eyes. He was witty and charming and he made her laugh with his clever mimicry of customers and their oddities. She cracked up when he mimicked their baleful supervisor who prophesied 'dare' consequences for anyone not meeting the sales target for the month.

He had invited her to the movies a few times. But Sandhya had always made some excuse and wriggled out of the invitation. Though she liked him, these days she couldn't bring herself to go out with someone so, well, ordinary. To do that would have been an act of betrayal against her other life where men–high born and urbane like those glossy demigods in suit ads–stepped off their mansions and limousines and wooed her in magnificent ways.

Right now she was in the midst of a particularly intricate story that had been set off by a man she had encountered the day before yesterday. He was not exactly young, and he had come to the store with his wife. At least, Sandhya thought she was his wife. Usually, she avoided getting into stories with men who appeared to be married. She didn't like the complications that married men would bring to her story. But something about this man caught her off guard. She felt herself drawn to the way he grinned at her, baring his big, slightly yellow teeth, and the way the clumps of his black chest hair sprouted thickly from his open-necked shirt.

He was of medium height, with no hint of a belly, and was dressed casually in jeans and moccasins. A silver bracelet hung loose on his thick, hairy wrist, and he spoke to her courteously in a deep, well-modulated voice that made her feel less like a sales girl and more like his equal. His companion, one of those fortyish women who stay hard and trim, and whose faces seem to have stiffened with the effort, looked bored with his vacillations. "You make up your mind, sweetie," she told him, running her fingers through her lavishly streaked hair. "I'll go take a look at some eye make-up over there."

She wore black leggings and a yellow and black animal print top caught at the waist with a shiny black belt, and she clop-clopped away stiffly on her dagger like high heels. Sandhya thought the man looked a bit disappointed. But he grinned comically at her, as if to say, who's to argue with women, and concentrated on the scents she bore towards him like a slave girl bearing pitchers of aromatic water to a sultan's hamaam.

"Try this, Sir, it's a lovely citrus. Very cool and refreshing," Sandhya said softly, winningly. She was glad to be rid of the woman, and half surprised that her brain was already lunging into a brand new story. And as if he had sensed the visions beginning to take life behind her polite, interested eyes, the man placed one forearm on the counter, leaned forward and sideways, and said,

"Why don't you recommend something, hmm? I'll take what you suggest."

She sold him an expensive fragrance, of course. But she took care to do it with due ceremony–giving him several options and getting him to smell the coffee beans again and again.

"Rs 9050 for a 100ml bottle! It's criminal," he laughed, crinkling his broad, flattish nose. "But it's good, I agree. I'll take it."

By this time the woman had come back. She took a look at his selection, smiled indifferently, and said, "Mm. Nice. Let me buy it for you, daaling. It's for his birthday," she threw the last few words at Sandhya in an offhand way. Sandhya immediately snapped on her thrilled-excited look and said "oh", as though she had heard an amazing piece of good news.

The man and the woman melted into the Saturday afternoon crowd. But by then Sandhya had claimed them as characters in the ever-sprouting drama of her vivid imaginary life.

The man progressed quickly in her head, changing from a rich businessman with a roving eye to a heavy-drinking misanthrope (with no diminution in his wealth, naturally) who found he could unburden himself to her. He had a hell of a marriage, he told her. He had loved his wife to distraction, but she had treated him like dirt and had slept with his best friend. He had so wanted a child, yet she had refused to have one because she did not want to lose her freedom. (This sounded a bit idiotic, Sandhya admitted, because everyone knew that rich women never lost their freedom after having a baby. But at this point she could not think of a better reason for the woman not to have wanted a child.) Though he wished to end the marriage now, he hesitated to file for a divorce as it would lead to a lot of muckraking. These days he couldn't sleep without downing several glasses of alcohol, he told her while driving her home. (The men in her stories always drove her home at night). He was a bitter, broken man, she realised, and he was letting himself go to pieces. Sandhya couldn't help but sympathise with him. Yet she didn't want to have too much to do with him. His cynical, bloodshot eyes scared her a little. She hoped he wasn't attracted to her. She wanted to be his friend, nothing more...

And today, when business was dull this Monday morning, and the sales girls and boys stood chatting in little groups, she brought him out and thought him up some more. She imagined going out for dinner with him. It was at one of those expensive places where the lights were so dim that you couldn't read the menu. She had put on her best dress—the short, black, backless designer knock-off that she kept locked in her trunk and had never dared to wear in real life. She was also wearing her teardrop pearl earrings and the gleaming, high-heeled, ankle-length boots that she had got at a fantastic discount at the store. She could see that Arjun (she had names for all her leading men) was impressed. He told her that he wanted to see her more often. He held her hand. His silver bracelet felt cold where it touched her, but his lips were hot when he pressed them to her throat. "I don't want glamour, I want feeling. I want love," he murmured...

From the corner of her eye Sandhya saw Abhishek make his way towards her. She pulled herself back from her reverie and let out a silent groan. He had called her this morning. She had let the phone ring away.

"*Aei* Sandy," he demanded good-naturedly, "Why didn't you take my call today?"

She liked it that he called her Sandy instead of Sandhya. She felt the name suited her. These days some of the others had also started calling her that, though one girl had said tartly, "Let's not call her Sandy, that's Abhishek's special name for her."

Sandhya turned her calm face to Abhishek and said, "Oh, I didn't hear the phone ring. Then I thought I'd find out what it was about when I met you and not waste a call."

He wanted to know if she was going to their colleagues' wedding reception that night. Of course, she said. They had been talking about it for days. It was a department store romance, after all. There had been no end of excitement about it.

"I'll drop you home if you need a lift," he said. "I've borrowed my brother-in-law's car," he said in an excited voice.

"You know how to drive?"

"Sure. My brother-in-law taught me. I passed the test last year," he said proudly. "In fact, I often drive my brother-in-law's car. I plan to have a car one day."

Sandhya was pleased. But she said coolly, "Oh, there'll be others going that way. We were planning to take a taxi, you don't have to drop me."

"I want to," he said, looking into her eyes.

It was almost 10 o'clock by the time the group from the department store reached the wedding hall. They had had to wait till it was nearly closing time before they could start getting ready for the occasion. The girls had changed into silk sarees and put on bits of jewellery. The men were dressed in their best clothes too. When they arrived the wedding ceremony was over, but the lateness of the hour did little to dampen their jollity. The outing was a rare treat and they intended to make the most of it. The bride and the groom were seated on their red velvet thrones and were receiving the last guests with tired smiles. They too perked up when they saw their colleagues. There was much joking and laughing for a while, and even their dour supervisor relaxed and teased the groom about the danger of not making the cut on this crucial bridal night. Then the little party stood like jubilant guards on either side of the newlyweds as the videographer trained an unending beam of white hot light upon them and sought to capture the moment forever.

They were soon shepherded into the eating area. It was late and they were being gently urged to finish their dinner. Sandhya, resplendent in a green and gold saree, wondered idly what Arjun would have said to her had he seen her now. But she had no time to pursue that line of thought. She was in the midst of a noisy melee, surrounded by her boisterous colleagues who were throwing loud jests at each other as if the place belonged to them. And oh, did they have to pile their plates with such indecent amounts of food, Sandhya winced inwardly. It made them look so greedy and low—like a gaggle of famished peasants! She picked daintily at her fish fry, shamed by the inelegant gluttony of her colleagues, yet taking care to laugh at their jokes from time to time.

"So who's next in line to be married from our mall marriage bureau?"

"I can make a guess," someone said. Preeti, the girl with the shrillest voice in the company, cried, "No, no, keep quiet, let me say it—I'll say it."

Sandhya held her smile and moved away slightly. All these girls she worked with were marriage-mad, she thought contemptuously. They were just waiting to get married! They didn't seem to realise that the excitement lay in the possibilities rather than the actual event. It occurred to her fleetingly that the possibilities she played with in her head, if taken to their wished-for conclusion, did culminate in marriage. But no, she was not like the others, she told herself. Her mother had hesitatingly asked her one day if she had met any nice boys at the department store. She had given her a sharp, outraged retort, as if her mother had suggested that she prostitute herself like those shadowy whores who waited on Kalighat bridge while the river below flowed darkly with its flotsam of refuse. Marry one of the boys at the department store! The very idea! She didn't tell her mother that she was meant for something finer. She would choose someone powerful and elevating, someone who would open the world for her and make her see its wonders. She wanted to travel! See the Great Barrier Reef and the Aurora Borealis! She wanted to go white water rafting! And savour the exotic foods they showed on television! She wanted sensation and drama and all the maddening, breathtaking strangeness and sweetness that the world had to offer. And she was looking for a way. She was tunnelling through the love stories in her head to take her someplace else. She was riding the roads to her idyll. The only thing that she hadn't figured out yet was the nature of that idyll and the scent it would give off. Would it be a cloying floral, or a sunny, sylvan thing? Or would she rather be seduced by a heavy-lidded musk that pulled her into deep unknowable woods?

"Why are you so quiet," Abhishek said, butting into her dreams. "By the way, you're looking really pretty tonight," he added shyly.

She flashed him a smile and muttered a muted "thanks". She had noticed that he hadn't taken as much food on his plate as some of the other men had, and she liked him for it. Abhishek wasn't a bad guy, she decided. But she didn't really want to be here with him. In fact, she didn't want to be here at all. She was impatient to get away now, away from her colleagues, away from the fast emptying marriage hall—already forlorn and smelling of spent flowers and echoing with the rough clatter of plastic chairs being stacked away. She wanted to get back where she really belonged, the thrilling space in her head, where Arjun, the tormented soul, waited for her to grant him a wish.

When they finally left to the mighty clanging of the caterer's men gathering up their stuff, it was close to midnight. They broke up into little groups according to the area where they lived and began to look for cabs. Sandhya and three others were taking a lift in Abhishek's borrowed car. He dropped them off one by one until only he and Sandhya were left in the car.

"You better come and sit in the front. Otherwise people will think I am your driver," Abhishek said with an embarrassed laugh.

Obediently, Sandhya got out of the back seat and went and sat beside him in the front.

Abhishek drove slowly, as if he did not want the journey to end. They were sailing up a bridge now. And though the road was pot-holed, and the railings of the bridge twisted and bent, Sandhya felt they were climbing a magical swell that glowed softly beneath the yellow street lamps. It was so, so mysterious, she thought, so full of the unknown! Was that gold dust on the asphalt, she thought, swooning a little, and where was this man taking her, on and on over this burnished path? Then they crossed the bridge and came down and mingled once more with the desultory snapshots of midnight—the overloaded truck grinding through the silence, a yellow cab being washed by a tireless young man, and vagrants huddled in sleep under the smoggy, wakeful sky.

Abhishek was making small talk. Sandhya replied in monosyllables. It struck her that one of her most done and overdone fantasies, that of being dropped home in a car by a man who was in love with her, was sort of happening right now. And yet, incredibly, she took no delight in it.

When Abhishek brought the car to a halt next to the sidewalk in an ill-lit lane, she was assailed by a sense of déjà vu and flooded with visions of a hundred other assignations in a hundred other ill-lit lanes. Only, it was not meant to be thus, she thought, and tensed her body to fight off this interloper into her splendorous phantom life.

Then a black sedan came from the opposite direction and stopped in front of them a little distance away. A man got out. A woman's arm, phosphorescent under the street light, snaked out of the window and waved to him. The man waved back. The light caught something shiny on his wrist and it flashed like a beacon for a moment before the man turned and vanished into the maw of the night.

Arjun! That was Arjun, Sandhya thought with a start. Arjun! The man with the bracelet who touched her softly and suffered so deeply! Oh yes, she was sure it was him! But was this shadowy image (who had perhaps lain entwined with that woman in the car) the real man or the one she had summoned in her dreams? She found that she couldn't tell which was which anymore. Her two worlds—the real and the fantastical—collided and knocked her out. She saw herself banished from her perfumed garden, her garden of fragrant dreams, and she clutched at the straws of the here and now, at the man who was saying "I love you" so predictably. When he pressed her hand, she was quiescent, unresisting. Emboldened, he moved closer, so close that the whites of his eyes filled her vision. She let him kiss her, and felt the waters under the Kalighat bridge close over her head.

The Kill

He stands by the peepul tree sipping tea from a small plastic cup. He takes tiny sips to make the tea last, letting the steam from it warm his chilly nose. It is early morning. A cold sun rose some time ago, but it gives little light. All you see is a haze—a dense, powdery smokiness that films the sun, slides off the lamp posts and the tree tops and creeps into you, slowly burrowing into your veins. Moisture clings darkly to the tufts of grass on the pavement. And the frosty air holds its breath. In an hour or two the sun may throw off its shroud. For now, the peepul tree looks misty blue and the houses across the street seem dull and faint.

Rohit doesn't mind standing in the sunless cold. He is young and strong. He can take the cold. Besides, he is nicely wrapped up. He wears a dirty red scarf that goes over his ears and around his head, a grey sweater and the padded black wind cheater he bought for 1200 rupees last winter. He wears his trousers over his pyjamas for added warmth and two pairs of socks, their holes roughly darned by himself. His black laced shoes are dusty, but they are a good, sturdy pair and none too worse for the wear.

He stands there, with one hand shoved deep inside his wind cheater pocket and the other holding the warm plastic cup close to his chin. His breath mingles with the steam and comes out in wispy white gusts. When the tea is finished, he tosses the cup with some regret. He can hear the sounds from the tea stall nearby—the hiss of the enormous aluminium kettle coming to a boil, the scrape-scrape of pots and pans being scrubbed, the desultory chat of the few customers who are here at this early hour. He feels like having another cup of tea. But he decides against it. The tea costs 5 bucks. He won't have another one just yet.

So he goes back to watching the house. It's a nondescript house, that No 8/37. Forlorn, down-at-heel, with paint curling off its dirt-streaked walls and bits of green sprouting from jagged, mossy cracks.

Kamal Shah and his family live on the ground floor. The first floor has just one small, asbestos-covered room. The rest of it is a bare, roofless expanse strung out with a few clotheslines. A solitary rope cot rests against its low walls. The neighbours know that the 8/37 people have been wanting to add rooms to the first floor for years. But they never have enough money to get the job done. Kamal Shah has a large family to support—a son away in college, a daughter at school, his parents and wife. He is a member of the ill-paid, overburdened middle class with a list of must-dos and appearances to keep up. He is making sure that his children get a decent education. He has fitted his parents' bedroom with an AC recently. He tries to do his duty and pay his dues. He tries to put by a little every month. But more often than not, his government clerk's salary quickly drains away. There is always some unforeseen expense to take care of.

So the Shahs do talk often about building rooms on the first floor, but they talk about it the way they might discuss plans of a holiday abroad. They know there is a wide chasm between the wish and its fulfilment.

Rohit knows Kamal Shah, of course. He has seen him hundreds, probably thousands of times, rushing off to work dressed in his brown trousers and white terylene shirt. Or, coming back home in the evenings with slow, tired steps. He is a small, melancholy man who looks as if he needs some rest. Rohit doesn't think he has ever spoken to him much. But he talks to his wife Reshma Bhabi whenever he goes to their house to pick up or deliver the ironed clothes. He has known the family since he was a boy, when his father used to be the local press*wala*. Since he died two years ago, Rohit has been running the ironing business. He is now the master of their red hot *chullah* and the smooth, flat irons that he thwacks again and again on the clothes until every crease and wrinkle disappears and the clothes are folded in sharp, neat stacks.

It will soon be time again to fire up the *chullah* and start the day's work. Rohit hopes Chhotu, his assistant, will do it. But the lazy bastard rarely starts work unless shouted at and told to get a move on. He curses under his breath. In a bit, he will have to leave his watch and go back to his ironing shed. You simply can't leave things to that rascal.

He needs to get back, he thinks impatiently. What is the purpose of standing here anyway?

No one told him to come here early in the morning today. And in this wretched cold too! Yet, waking up at 6 as he always does, he was assailed by such a sense of heart-hammering disquiet that he felt he had to come here. He sprang out of his cot, dressed, made a hurried visit to the latrine and swiftly crossed the two lanes that separated Kamal Shah's house and the *jhuggi* where he and his mother lives. His mother, indiscernible under layers of rags and a threadbare blanket, was snoring uproariously when he left.

Hey Bhagwaan, they had all been so angry last night! Raghu, Hukam, Krishna, Bhairon and he! They sat around a little fire made up with coal and bits of wood and dry leaves, toasting their hands over its crackling orange flames. Their faces glowed in the firelight and their eyes flashed like animals on the prowl.

"How dare they," spat Bhairon. "Those fucking sons of whores!"

"Those dirty bastards are insulting us–all of us," Hukam said, trembling with outrage.

"They are doing it on purpose," nodded Krishna, stroking his moustache thoughtfully. "They are polluting everything, the neighbourhood itself!"

"But we don't have proof..." hesitated Raghu.

"What more proof do we need, brother," Hukam turned on him indignantly. "Chhotu overheard Kamal Shah's mother talking when he went to their house this afternoon."

Yes, and their maid, that Chameli who does their dishes, suspects it too," nodded Bhairon.

"We won't allow it," Krishna said, grinding his teeth. "By god, we won't!

They are not exactly bosom friends, but they know each other well. Bhairon is an auto driver; Hukam has a fruit stall on the main road; Raghu, the peanut seller, is the poorest of the lot and Krishna, the electrician, is the most well-to-do and by common consent, the most well-informed.

They are local boys and men who sometimes get together in twos and threes to have *chai-pakore*. They exchange *mohalla* gossip and talk about the wheelings and dealings at the council. Who made a killing. Who got gulled. Who took how much *rishwat*. They also keep their eyes and ears open for any immoral hanky panky going on in the neighbourhood. Dirty deals are one thing.

They're a part of life. But illicit, *galat* stuff happening between men and women cannot be tolerated.

So there's always plenty of talk on the street that goes well with *chai-pakore*. Or with glasses of cheap liquor that singe their throats and set their spirits blazing. Sitting at a dimly-lit *theka* of an evening, they may watch a bit of porn on Krishna's big-screen phone and whistle and crack lewd jokes.

But all this is just time-pass. They are always sombre and grave when it comes to the really important stuff. Stuff like religion or morality. Although none of them is particularly religious or particularly moral, they set an awful lot of store by these things. It's like honour. They could die for it. Perhaps they could kill for it.

This matter about the Shahs, for example. It had to be tackled. Did those people have no fear? Didn't they know they were playing with fire? Well, they'd show them what comes of crossing the line.

"We have to teach them a lesson. A very harsh lesson," Hukam exclaimed, not for the first time.

"Has Chhotu talked to anyone else," Bhairon asked.

"He may have," Rohit said carelessly. "The rascal goes gossiping around the entire *mohalla*. I can hardly get him to do any work."

"So. The news will spread," Krishna said. "Who knows, it may have spread already. I must speak with Councillor Singh*ji*. He will know what to do. *Iski sazaa milni chahiye.*"

There was a grim chorus of approval.

"*Zaroor. Zaroor milni chahiye.*"

"Shall we inform the police too," Rohit asked.

"No, *bhai*," Bhairon said. "There are a thousand hassles when you involve the police. Krishna *bhai* is right. We must consult with Singh*ji*. Why not call him right now," he said and turned to Krishna.

"No, not now," Krishna said shortly. "He is with his mistress now."

They sniggered at this, their fury momentarily forgotten, as they pictured the sexagenarian Singh*ji* bouncing on some fleshy young woman.

"That fat old man," exclaimed Raghu, chuckling. "And horny as hell, eh?"

"Let be," Krishna said curtly. "Let's focus on this situation."

So they sent out WhatsApp messages to some others in the neighbourhood. Soon more people joined them. They were regular folk–shopkeepers, tradesmen, vendors. They were all god-fearing men mostly, and they were all trying to eke out a living in this drab, downbeat locality where development has devolved into smart phones. Some had heard the rumour already. News spreads fast in this slow *mohalla*, whispers swirl and gather pace like an angry dust storm.

The fire had gone out. Only the cinders glowed and smoked. But they stood there, reluctant to leave this spot of fast-fading warmth. The cold night air stung their eyes and made them water. They rubbed their hands, coughed, grew hoarse and spat.

Every day they flailed vainly at a thousand injustices. Every day they felt defeated and done in. But not this time. They had agency this time. This was one assault on their common dignity they could retaliate against. They would avenge this abomination! Those stinking immoral Shahs! They would show them! They bubbled in their wrath as the crescendo of their ferocious whispers rose like the wing flaps of a giant night bird. They were a shabby band of men, but their blood was up and they grew immense and strong, itching to hand out a sentence, itching to execute it at once.

"Who knew that Kamal Shah would turn out to be such a mother-fucking scoundrel! What a devious, vile little man," exclaimed Ramji who works at the grocery store. "By the way, he is always trying to get out of paying his bills. He owes thousands. Thousands."

They knew this wasn't true. No one had ever heard that Kamal Shah owed anyone money. But right now they didn't want to nitpick about such things. So Ramji continued. The little silver ring he wore in one ear glinted in the dark.

"And his wife. What about her? She is Hindu, they say. That rotten bastard has already ruined one Hindu family. Maybe he kidnapped her and then married her! *Saaley*! He has been playing with our honour for years!"

"Yes, she's Hindu. That's what people say. *Oye* Rohit, remember you told me that one day?"

Rohit nodded. Many years ago he had once heard Reshma Bhabi say "*Hey prabhu*". That clinched her religion for him. She is one of us, he had thought joyfully. It made him like her even more. Rohit had always been fond of her. As a boy he used to think she looked like a fairy from heaven. He tried not to stare at her milky skin and her rosy finger tips with which she handed him the money for the ironed clothes.

"Yes, she is Hindu," he said a little loudly now, as though he wanted to place her outside their flaming circle of rage.

They would have gone to Kamal Shah's house right then. But Krishna and Ramji demurred. "We have to consult the local leaders, the *poltishuns*. It could get complicated. They understand how to do these things. We must proceed carefully," said Krishna.

"Right," Ramji agreed. "We must get more people too. Hundreds. Thousands. They'll all come. When they hear what has happened, they will come. And then we can go and beat the shit out of those sister-fuckers!"

Rohit has been watching the house for almost an hour, as though he expects it to reveal its terrible secret in this cold morning light. Of course, we have good reason to be angry, he thinks defensively. It's unforgivable, what they've done, going against the natural law, sinning against all that's sacred...And yet and yet....

Since last night his fury has ebbed and flowed, at times giving way to a dread that envelops him like this foul winter mist. What if they are wrong? What if Chhotu misinterpreted what Kamal Shah's mother was talking about? That boy has a hyperactive imagination after all. He's always making up stories. And even if it's true, what will they do to Kamal Shah and his family? To Reshma Bhabi? And Raushni, their 17-year-old daughter, who is lovely as a spring day? He has watched her grow as he grew from boy to man. He is 24 now, time for him to get married, his mother says. But he baulks at marriage. Not just yet, he says.

Sometimes he comes upon Raushni and looks at her discreetly. She really is like a burst of *raushni*, he thinks, a current of miraculous light. When she walks by with her serene, radiant face held high over the ivory column of her throat, he feels an exquisite spasm, a quickening in his blood that he tells no one about.

Oh, he wishes it had been over last night when there was no time to think. They could have gone to the police or landed up at Kamal Shah's place and maybe slapped him around a bit. One slap and it would have put the fear of god into that thin, mousy man! It would have taught him a lesson he'd never forget! But now who knows what might happen?

He imagines Krishna, Ramji and others going to the leaders. He pictures them sitting and planning the details of this operation. They will amass more people, oh yes, they will. By evening people from near and far will turn up here to punish Kamal Shah and his family for their sin.

Should he warn them? Should he knock on that rickety blue-painted door of No 8/37 and tell Kamal Shah to take his family and run? Rohit knows a part of him wants to do just that. Kamal Shah, his father and mother can go hang, but there is Reshma Bhabi and Raushni to think of.

The morning is opening up now. And little by little the haze rolls away under the diffident sun. There are more people on the road and the usual sounds of a brand new day. An e-rickshaw sputters by, carrying its cage of school children. They look like warm little bundles dressed in their navy blue woollens and bright woolly caps. Their cheeks are dry and ruddy in the cold. A man pushes a cycle-cart filled with winter vegetables that gleam like jewels. He calls out as he goes—a sonorous ditty of *mooli-palak-gobi-tamatar* that rings high and clear in the morning air. A smell of smoke wafts in from somewhere, bringing with it the aroma of parathas sizzling in ghee.

The smell sparks a memory in Rohit.

He remembers Reshma Bhabi feeding him biryani on Eid days. The biryani tasted so good! The long and fragrant ghee-soaked rice; the chunks of meat, dark, flavourful and succulent. He smiles at the memory, remembering how he would long for a second helping. And then Reshma Bhabi, in her clairvoyant way, would serve it to him without being asked. She often gave him something to eat when he went to their house in the evenings to deliver the ironed clothes. He remembers sitting with her son Azad and eating *phirni* and kheer made with delicate threads of *sewaiyan*. And Bhabi's kababs—they were so soft that they melted in the mouth. She had once asked his father if it was all right for Rohit to eat at their place sometimes. His father, a humble man with a generous heart and a loud belly laugh, had said, of course it was. Wasn't every religion the same deep down? "You are like a mother to Rohit. It is his good fortune that someone like you is fond of him," he had said.

But then the ritual stopped at some point. Rohit doesn't recall exactly when or why. Maybe he just grew up. He grew up, dropped out of school in the 9th standard, and one day, politely declined when Reshma Bhabi offered him a plate of something or the other.

Standing at his observation post under the peepul tree, Rohit fidgets. He is usually not given to indecision. And here he is in this grave *dharamsankat*, a moral dilemma. What nonsense, he scolds himself at once. *Bakwaas*! Where's the dilemma? They did something terrible—that Kamal Shah and his family. They must be taught a good lesson! Then why is he standing here like a village idiot dithering and debating? He takes out his phone from the pocket of his jacket and looks at the time. It's 7.30. Soon, someone will spot him and ask why he is loitering here. He can say that he is watching to make sure that Kamal Shah doesn't run away. But that will sound pretty lame. Besides, not everyone knows that Kamal Shah needs watching, or that he might run away.

And then he sees the blue door of 8/37 opening and Raushni stepping out.

He feels that familiar dizzy tingling in his scalp when he sees her. She is dressed in her school uniform—bottle green cardigan, blazer and skirt and green stockings. She walks towards him now. Her step is carefree and light, as though she were going to a dance. Her forehead is bright as a mirror and her night-black hair is tied in a long plait that hangs down her front. Her satchel swings against her hips as she walks.

She looks straight ahead, seeing and not seeing, and her coral lips suddenly break into a smile. For one ecstatic, heart-stopping moment Rohit thinks she is smiling at him. Then he realises that she has probably thought of something amusing. It's a secret little smile, a moment of private joy, but it makes the morning jubilant and thrilling.

And in that instant Rohit understands why he is here. He understands that he has come out at this early hour so he can see Raushni when she goes to take a bus to her school. He has come to find out if the sight of her can change the course of today. His heart swells and lurches painfully into his throat. She is near him now. He hears the swish of her skirt and feels the air rippling at her approach. He takes a step forward to tell her what he can. He has to whisper it quickly, urgently. He doesn't know what he will say, but in a moment, he will.

Raushni stops. She is startled to see Rohit blocking her way. They look at each other–he speechless, she astonished, incredulous. Then another expression flits across her face. And sidestepping him neatly, she walks on as if nothing has happened.

At once he too turns around and walks away, yanking off the scarf around his head and pulling down the zipper of his wind cheater with a vicious rip.

He feels hot suddenly. Hot, lumpy and ill-dressed. His rage is like a red mist before his eyes and he can barely see. Her look burns in his brain, the look of contempt and pity, of faint distaste at the audacity of small men.

By nightfall they have started gathering two streets away. The local leaders have planned this well.

The news has been skilfully spread, the rumours affirmed, inflated and embellished. The fire has been lit and stoked and their fury is a roaring conflagration now. The crowd stirs and heaves, like red-eyed bulls raring to run and gore. They have come from all over, some from places a few hours' train ride away. It's a just cause after all. Justice must be done.

"Brothers, they have eaten the forbidden flesh," thunders the councillor, Singh*ji*. "Who knows, they may be eating it as we speak. They have slaughtered our beloved *gau mata* and devoured her. They've made their unclean biryani and beef kababs. Shall we let them commit this heinous crime against our religion? Shall we let them defile our *mohalla*," he cries.

No! They shriek in response and a hundred fists rise up and punch the air.

Maaro, maaro, beat them, kill them, snarl the *rakshaks*, the cow protectors. Their eyes burn with sacred hate and they raise their sticks heavenwards as though they were seeking divine benediction upon their holy war.

"What're we waiting for," a woman screams shrilly.

"They know it's a crime. They know it's a sin. Yet they have done it to make a mockery of our religion and our laws," cries the local party leader. "What shall we do to them?"

"Beat the bastards, kill the sons of whores," they howl, beginning to move already.

A cold wind whips around them, but they barely feel it. They are fused in their frenzy, turned into a headless mass of blood and sinew that surges forward and seeks more blood.

Rohit surges with the mob and thinks of nothing.

The Love Song of Maya K

The cafe was noisy and over-crowded. It was one of those places frequented by the slightly older set who liked to breeze in after browsing around the bookshop that was adjacent to it. It was tiny, cramped and borderline shabby. Its menu, though, was cool and pricey—which was good, because the people who dropped by liked the twinning of shabby with pricey. It made the cafe feel classy-casual, which was how they liked to think of themselves too. They were regular folk, of course, but they had an air of knowingness about them that set them apart from the clueless janta—the kind who shopped at Sarojini Nagar or went to Shimla for a holiday.

Here the people were earnest and passionate about things that mattered. They talked about the way the cultural narrative was changing in India. They discussed the Maoist movement in Bastar with occasional switchbacks to their latest travels in Croatia or Vietnam. Huddled around the small green wooden tables, they picked at their organic salads or gluten-free pizzas and sipped cold-pressed juices while they discussed stuff and agreed with each other. You didn't disagree with your companions in places like these. You were either on the same wavelength or fast getting there.

Jamila had introduced Maya to this cafe. It wasn't quite Maya's kind of place, as she wasn't into organic salads and cold-pressed juices. She also didn't give a damn about the radicalisation of the people of Bastar. She had caught snatches of such talk more than once when she used to come here with Jamila. On one occasion, she had exclaimed loudly, "Dude, if you care about the people of Bastar, DO something about them instead of pontificating over your pomegranate juice!"

The Bastar bleeding-hearts at the next table had pretended to be deaf while Jamila had giggled and shushed her.

And here Maya was again today, waiting to meet Jamila like old times.

She took a quick look around the cafe. Not a single table free and Jamila wasn't here yet. She stood near the entrance, one leg slightly bent at the knee, looking like a wannabe model in her big hair, long burgundy H&M coat, white woollen jumper, skinny jeans, and black suede ankle length boots. Wasn't winter in Delhi just lovely, thought Maya, who worked in a fashion house as an assistant merchandise manager. You could dress chic here, dress like the *firangs*! Back where she came from, in the steamy peninsula of the south, there were only three seasons–hot, hotter, hottest.

She noticed a white man sitting alone at a corner table. Seeing that he was looking at her, she let her eyes lock into his for a few seconds. Then she looked away, fluffing up her hair with her hand as she did so, pleased that he was still watching her.

The cafe door swung open with a clang and Maya flinched. A man with a beard and a worn laptop bag hanging from his shoulders came in and left the moment he saw that all the tables were taken. She wondered if she should follow suit and message Jamila to meet her at another coffee shop down the same road. Then she saw a woman signalling for her check. So she waited some more. But the woman and her two male friends dawdled over the dregs of their coffee, impervious to Maya's pointed looks.

She felt foolish standing there like a mannequin that had lost its way while others came, surveyed the scene and went away, making the entrance door clang again and again like a startled temple bell.

Jamila showed up almost at the exact instant when she finally got the table.

"Hello, Maya," she said.

"Aren't you lucky," Maya said, pursing her lips and smiling. "I waited 15 minutes to get this table. And as soon as I get it, you land up."

"I tried to come sooner," Jamila said with a hint of apology. "But tough getting away from work early. And then there's the traffic."

"So what's up," she asked. "Why the flurry of messages?"

Ignoring the faint chill in Jamila's tone, Maya gestured to the waiter.

"Do you want to share a goat cheese pizza?"

"Gluten-free?" Jamila asked with a slight smile.

"Ha ha. Over my dead body," Maya exclaimed, laughing.

"I'm not very hungry." Jamila said. "But sure, I can have a bite. I haven't been here since the last time I came with you."

They ordered the pizza and two Americanos. They had similar tastes in caffeine, if not in food.

"We could share a dessert later," Maya said, sounding as if she wanted to make it up to her for forcing her to agree to the pizza.

When the waiter left, Maya dimpled at Jamila and said, "Hey, you're looking good! I don't know how you manage to wear a saree even in cold weather."

Jamila smiled and said nothing.

She was a woman with a rare gift of stillness. She could remain quiet, calmly looking on as the conversation flowed over and around her. Remoteness was her default position, an aristocratic self-possession her natural state. She rarely spoke if she did not feel like it, and often chose not to answer half queries and observations that were directed at her. It made people think that she was rude and stuck-up. But Jamila didn't care. If the mood took her, she gathered herself close, folded herself layer upon layer like a flower in the night, and became silent and inscrutable as a goddess.

"How do you do it, Jammy," Maya had said to her once. "How do you manage to be so quiet around people and not feel the pressure to say anything? I start babbling out of pure embarrassment lest people think I am dumb or have nothing meaningful to say."

And look at Jamila now, Maya said to herself, sitting there cucumber-cool as always, her oval Madonna head slightly inclined, her eyes pooling unfathomably. She was coldly luminous in her violet silk saree and dove grey coat. Her *pallu* was looped like a scarf around her throat and her long hair was twisted into a low-slung knot. She looked as serene as a nun and as aloof, and her tip-tilted fingers were clasped in an attitude of concentration or prayer.

"I broke up with Sudeep," Maya declared abruptly.

Jamila raised one finely arched brow.

"Oh," she said.

"It wasn't working out," Maya said. "He had become way too possessive and overbearing. He was watching my every move. I felt stifled."

Jamila said nothing.

"I think he is stalking me."

At this Jamila smiled. "Come on, don't be dramatic. I have met Sudeep—he's hardly the obsessive stalker type."

"He's a schizoid prick. Totally obsessive."

"Really? Well, that's quite a change from what you said eight months ago," Jamila said, smiling her small, sardonic smile. "If I remember right, you said he was perfect. You said you saw a future in this relationship."

"I did, didn't I," Maya said bitterly, twirling the salt and pepper mills round and round between her fingers.

Jamila and Maya had little in common. Yet they had become friends after a chance meeting at a classical music concert three years ago. She was a recent migrant to the Capital then, and Jamila, older to her by four years, had taken her under her wing. She had introduced her to people and given her tips on finding her feet in a new city. Maya had been a little dazzled by the attention. She was Maya K, the small town girl with earthy looks and wild hair, whereas Jamila Ansari was old money–part of the city's smart, entitled crowd. Her parents knew ministers past and present and lived amidst the lush sweep of Lutyens' Delhi in a big house with a lawn and three dogs of expensive breeds. Jamila did not live with them. At some point in her adult life she had moved out. She now stayed in an apartment on the other side of the foul sludge of the Yamuna. It was convenient because the architect's firm where she worked was not far from where she lived. What her apartment and its environs lacked in prettiness, they made up for in the freedom they afforded her to conduct her life as she pleased.

"You're serious?" Jamila asked now. "Sudeep is actually stalking you because you broke up with him?"

She kept her voice low, so the people at the next table wouldn't get to listen in. But she needn't have bothered. Maya spoke loudly and clearly, not caring a whit as to who heard her.

"Yes, I'm pretty sure he is. After I split with him three weeks ago, he kept sending me messages, saying he loved me, that he would give me more space, not try to impose his views on me, etc.

He kept calling me too. To be honest, I was in two minds—part of me didn't really want to break up with him, you know."

Jamila remained silent.

Maya went on: "So anyway, he started making such a nuisance of himself, calling me at all odd hours, at work and all that I finally realised that I had taken the right decision. He can't take no for an answer! A total control freak, wants to totally control my life! When he realised that I wasn't going to change my mind, he started threatening me. He sent messages saying stuff like 'You'll be sorry', 'You hurt me, and you'll get hurt too'. Crap like that."

"That could be just dumped-lover talk, no?"

"Yeah, but listen to this. A couple of nights back I had gone partying with some friends and he sent a message the next morning, saying, 'Had fun last night? I know all about you, you slut.'

"That's when I really freaked out. How did he know about the party? I'm now convinced that he is stalking me. Or he has got someone to do it."

Jamila noticed that she said "freagedout". Though Maya had sanded down her provincial accent to a stub, it slipped out now and then when she was agitated.

"Well, maybe someone at the party mentioned it to him. You have common friends," said Jamila.

"Not at this party, no. Completely different crowd. Only just met the guy who took me to this do."

"Only just met?" Jamila said softly, raising an eloquent brow.

"Oh, please!" Maya rolled her eyes. "Don't you start now!"

The pizza arrived. Jamila pushed the plate towards Maya.

"Have a bit, no?" Maya said. "I'm super hungry"

She wolfed down three-quarters of the pizza, barely tasting anything and taking comfort only in the warm weight of the food sliding down her gullet and settling into her stomach.

"This is so good," she sighed as Jamila nibbled her slice of pizza. "So what do you think?"

"Well, obviously, this is serious–that is, if he is really stalking you or having you stalked," Jamila said. Her impassive face was rearranging itself into an expression of concern.

"Have you told anyone?"

"No, just you. All my other friends think Sudeep is a fabulous guy–smart, funny, eligible–the works. They think I was a fool to break up with him. They wouldn't believe me if I told them that Sudeep is really a deranged stalker."

"You have the messages, right? You can report him to the police. In fact, you should."

"I've thought about that. But I don't know what that involves. Do I have to file a case against him? Would the police go and warn him? Would it make things worse? I mean, if I ignore it, he might get tired of this and give up. Or should I write a letter to his HR department? But that could make him even more vengeful, no? And then I think, God, what if he hires some guy to throw acid on me? He's a coward, he'd never do it himself, but he could always get someone to do it, right? Acid *dalneka supaari*! It's fucking scary, man!"

She was talking fast now, her voice scratchy and high, her words tumbling out in a rush.

"Maya, please calm down," Jamila said. "I'm sure Sudeep wouldn't do anything so...so...extreme. He's not some loser with nothing to lose–he has a fancy job, he earns lots. Why should he risk all that? He is too smart and careful to get involved in a crime. Listen, you know my friend Meenal–the lawyer? She handles a lot of women's cases–domestic violence, sexual harassment and all. I'll call her today and ask her for her advice."

"Will you? That would be great. I do need some expert advice. This guy is mindfucking me."

"That's a new word to me," Jamila said with a small chuckle.

Maya grimaced. "But it totally describes what he's doing to me, right?"

By the time she left the cafe, Maya felt her spirits rising. She had been hesitant about confiding in Jamila. They had not been in touch since their falling out eight months ago. She had said nasty things to her back then. But Jamila hadn't held a grudge. She had been sympathetic and kind and their conversation had quickly settled into the easy groove of their old friendship, as if there had been no hiatus at all.

She felt relieved that she had finally told someone about this crazy business. For it *was* crazy! This wasn't some unknown psycho who was stalking her—this was Sudeep, the suave, ambitious corporate high flyer. Guys like him weren't supposed to do sick stuff like this! That is why she had not told anyone else about it. The friends who knew him would think she was paranoid. They would dismiss his creepy messages and say that he had taken the break-up badly. Give him some time, they would say, he'll get over it and move on.

But Jamila was different. She knew Jammy would understand. You could always count on Jammy. Sometimes she thought Jammy understood her better than she did herself. Jammy knew she could be callous and callow, terrible and naive, as given to wounding as she was to being wounded. And she did not judge her for it. "You're hard and prickly on the outside and all mushy and mixed-up inside," Jamila had once told Maya, lightly touching the untamed tumult of her hair. "Not a recipe for happiness," she had said, smiling slightly and shaking her head.

Maya buttoned up her coat against the chill wind and waited for the Uber she had summoned. The smog thickened, turning down the covers of the evening. Cars swished by, their headlamps painting the road with quick brushstrokes of light. A man and a woman were walking hand in hand. A girl in a short off-white coat with an outsize fur collar was advancing on her ruched high-heeled boots like a thin young stork. "I saw you, yaa," she cried into her phone. "I saw you with her!" Up ahead, two cops were standing stolidly near a police *chowki,* their khaki uniforms melting into the darkness. They muttered under their breaths and thumped the earth with their sticks. Not far from them, a bunch of ragged urchins played, their hair the colour of rust under the cold street light.

She watched the kids absently at first, and then with attention. They were at some sort of play, and the centre of it was a little girl, about six or seven, who sat crouched on a piece of stone on the pavement. The others surrounded her, taunting her and darting in to hit her now and then. They were mostly boys, but there were a couple of girls too. They jabbed and jeered at her and sang some unintelligible ditty. Again and again they recited their sing-song rhyme and ran in to strike her, howling with laughter as they did. And the little girl, dressed in tattered woollens like the rest of them, hid her face in the knobs of her small knees and cowered and whimpered.

For a moment Maya wondered if she should ask the cops to intervene. Then she decided against it. The cops barely glanced at the direction of the children. It was as if they witnessed this piece of theatre every single day. Besides, it wasn't up to her to try and stop the random brutality of the streets. When the cab arrived, she rode away and didn't think of the little girl again. Instead, a long-buried memory floated up into her brain. A dish of crisp-fried, spicy fish; her best friend Lalitha tempting her with it, and she taking a bite, thrilled with the taste of the forbidden flesh–hot, salty, smelling of the sea; her brother finding out and he and her cousins rounding on her; they spat at her for being an evil, unclean thing. And then the adults crashing upon her like the almighty storm that had once struck their coastline. Her father, a zealous Brahmin, had rolled up his *veshti* and proceeded to beat her with a piece of kindling. The others looked on as he thrashed her in the courtyard of their joint-family home. He struck her meticulously–going over her back, her arms, her shoulders, her buttocks, the backs of her thighs. By the time he was done, Maya had stopped screaming. But the welts on her flesh had screamed long and loud.

She broke out into a fever that night. Her parents left her to sweat it out, telling her with stony faces that God was punishing her for her sin.

She made up her mind to leave home right then. But she was 12 years old and it would be many more years before she finally did.

Driving back to her Noida apartment, Jamila felt oddly elated. A glow of satisfaction, a warm little flame of delight, burned pleasurably inside her. She was slightly ashamed that she should feel this way, but she acknowledged it without surprise. She had known Maya's infatuation with Sudeep wouldn't last. Maya was too good for him. Too bad it had taken her this long to find out.

The last time they met, they had looked at each other with hostility, both on the offensive, both dispensing with niceties that had seemed too bogus to be pursued.

"You don't find Sudeep arrogant and pompous," Jamila had said to Maya. "He seems like everything you're not. He has none of your spontaneity. None of your...your...honesty. I thought you had a built-in shit indicator—seems like it's packed up!"

"Oh, stop being so bloody sour," Maya had said. "You're wrong about Sudeep. He is kind, considerate, he is in love with me."

"And you with him?" Jamila had said, her voice dripping icicles.

"Yes!"

"Why? Because he's an IIT-IIM hot shot who checks all the right boxes?"

"What's wrong with that," Maya had shouted. "What's wrong with me wanting to marry someone like that?"

"Nothing at all. Except that this guy is dead wrong for you."

"You're jealous," Maya burst out. "You're trying to poison my mind about Sudeep! I have a real future with him—a proper future. I want to give it a shot, okay? So back off!"

"I will. Your starry-eyed conventionality is hardly a pleasant sight!"

"And it's best that we don't meet again," Maya exclaimed in fury.

"As you wish," Jamila said, already remote, already walling herself inside the architecture of her tightly-held emotions.

Maya had been only partly right, of course, Jamila thought as she let herself into her flat. She had been jealous, yes. But it was so much more than that.

The night Maya dumped Sudeep, he had been lolling naked on her red love seat, one long spindly leg hanging down its side and the other stuck up like a pole over the arm rest. It was an awkward posture but Sudeep looked perfectly at ease, as though he had been born into that pose. He had made himself a drink from Maya's meagre bar—a vodka tonic with a twist of lime—and the glass was balanced on his chest, spreading an aureole of moisture on his scattered chest hair.

A little while before, he had rolled off her and asked breathlessly, "That was good, no?"

"Mmm," she replied, feigning post-coital lassitude. Then she saw him looking at her with his slightly bulbous eyes, carefully examining her expression as though he wanted to pick up pathways to her brain. She immediately felt like telling him to fuck off and stop staring at her in that odd, intense fashion. But she did not. Instead, she nuzzled the nine o'clock bristle on his cheeks. "It was great," she sighed, hiding her face from him.

In truth, she had been growing ambivalent towards Sudeep for months. A sense of disquiet fringed her responses towards him. Yet though she felt her calm certitude and glowing confidence in him slowly slipping away, she baulked at breaking off the relationship. Heck, Jamila had been right! He did check all the right boxes. If one wished to get married—and why shouldn't she get married?—she could scarcely find a better candidate than Sudeep, who was decent looking and had a fancy job in a multi-national consultancy firm. She liked his solemn look of love and the way he protectively put his arm around her waist. She liked the fact that he was a good *catch*, though she loathed herself for participating in the vocabulary of women who look upon potential husbands as prey. She had reacted to Sudeep with a primitive biological snap—a fertile female magnetised by a male with bushels of social capital and good genes.

And she had been gratified with his response. Why not throw in the towel with this guy then, she had asked herself. Get married, settle down, have a couple of kids and do the stuff every woman her age seemed to want to do? Up until she met Sudeep, she didn't know if this was what she wanted. But his glittering eligibility made her almost cocky in her conviction that she had been wandering lost and directionless and had been found at last.

And even now, she couldn't make up her mind if her rapid disenchantment with Sudeep was because of what he was, or because of what she was. Perhaps it was her own quicksilver temper, an incorrigible trait in her character that sparked her discontent. She sensed that she was about to lose something keen and vital in herself, and doubted if the new adventure in her life would make up for the old. And that made her peevish. Her irritation with Sudeep was a slow burning wick, but it burned all the time, and she began to notice a hundred dark spots in his lustre. She began to feel that his self-assurance was really the most outrageous self-love and his optimism the insufferable gaiety of fools. She gritted her teeth each time he lifted a corner of his mouth and smiled as if he already knew all there was to know about whatever they were talking about. And she could barely conceal her annoyance when he spoke to her in a slightly authoritative tone. Did he think he was superior to her? Did he think she was an airhead? Did he *like* the idea of her as an airhead?

They had ordered Chinese food that night. While she was clearing the table of the remnants of her last meal and sundry other mess, Sudeep called out from his sofa cradle, naked as a baby and quite as unsubtle. "Hey, the table is meant for eating on, Babes. Why use it as a dumping ground?"

Maya threw him a furious look. He noticed nothing and continued: "By the way, we must discuss our visit to my parents' place next week. And, Babes, could you turn the heater towards me, I'm feeling a bit cold."

"Oh, get up and put something on," she snapped, arranging the place mats on the table. "You look silly lying there all naked."

He swung himself up then, looking at her with hurt eyes. As he dressed sulkily, she flared at him again.

"And what's to discuss? I'm just meeting your folks–why make such a song and dance about it?"

"You don't think this is important," he asked, annoyed now. "You need to dress and act in a certain way if you're going to make a good impression. You're their future *bahu*, after all."

At that Maya exploded. "Act in a certain way, dress in a *certain* way," she hollered, throwing down the place mats and looking around for something more substantial and breakable to hurl at him. Suddenly, she felt powerful and liberated–like a monster wave rising from the bowels of the sea. "I don't need to act, okay? I don't need to make a good impression! I'm not seeking a job with your fucking parents!"

They quarrelled violently. He called her a foul-mouthed bitch–selfish, sluttish and totally out of control; she said he was a control freak, tight-arsed and Talibanesque. She tried to punch him and he twisted her arm behind her back, hurting her quite a bit. It ended with her telling him to get out.

And, oh, the relief! The sweet relief of not having to make it work with this alpha male whom she wanted and did not want. Whom she thought she loved and knew she did not. The relief came mixed with anxiety, of course. She couldn't tell if she had taken a wrong turn, brought low again by her questing, conflicted nature–her hand forced to give the wheel of her life another mighty twirl so she came to stop at another place she did not quite choose. Sudeep's menacing messages and apparent stalking terrified her. And she imagined herself in varied scenes of assault. Knifed. Violated. Broken. Her skin charred. Her flesh melting. And she, her life flickering, her soul fleeing, lashed to her helplessness. Yet her grisly nightmares were also a validation of sorts. If Sudeep were a stalker, she had just taken the best decision of her life.

A week later, Maya was working at a presentation she was to make the next day. In between, she flirted showily with a male colleague, who had been attentive towards her for months, and whom she had not encouraged before. She dimpled at him and tossed her Medusa hair. When he made a feeble joke, she touched his arm and treated him to her special uncontrollable laughter. The man fairly swelled at the promise of half-glimpsed delights as Maya played with him like a boy plays with a rat and reflected idly on the colossal self-regard of men. After a while she lost interest, and when he came by and stood close to her desk, almost brushing against her, she got up and walked away. She had not received any more texts from Sudeep in the last few days. This had cheered her. Jamila's lawyer friend too had told her not to worry so much until she found any actual evidence of stalking. Of course, she could always file a police case against Sudeep for his threatening messages, the lawyer said. So Maya had become less afraid, less inclined to think that she was being pursued and hunted. In fact, she almost felt good thinking that in a sense, she too had power over Sudeep. She could, if she liked, drag his face through the dirt, puncture his reputation, prick the balloon of his ego. The very idea of it made her smile. But then, that too seemed like a useless bother and she began to wonder anew about what had been won and what lost. And if invisible eyes were watching her after all.

She was trying to wrap up her work quickly today. She was to go to Jamila's place for dinner this evening. Jamila had sent her a message earlier in the day, inviting her over. Maya had stared at the message for a long time. Then she briskly tapped out her reply: "Okay. Will be there by 8."

She headed out to Jamila's place straight from office. She was making this journey after many months, and everything seemed just as it was. The roads and intersections past Nizamuddin bridge were clotted as usual with vehicles and tired, homebound folks. They wanted to speed up and be off, but the road harnessed them to its own halting pace. Up above, the quick-falling night lay unseeing, bisected by its jewelled spine of street lamps. And the evil smog, which made frenzied headlines every day, obscured the way.

As she drew near her destination, Maya realised that she felt nothing at this moment—neither free nor tied to anything, neither centred not conflicted, neither a victim nor victorious. She was part of a trajectory, an arc of life, and she was stretched on that arch of pleasure and pain, carried along by a wave that troughed and crested again and yet again. I have always trusted my instincts, she said to herself. The rest is just society.

Jamila opened the door almost as soon as Maya rang the bell. It was as if she had been waiting for her by the door.

They hugged like old friends. Then Jamila took her by the hand and led her into her austere parlour.

"I'm sorry, Jammy," Maya whispered afterwards. She let Jamila take off her coat and unbutton her shirt. Her smooth breasts flew out like uncaged birds. Jamila touched them with wonder and gratitude. "It was a mistake...I was confused...I don't know..." Maya whispered again. She closed her eyes and tears rolled down her face.

Jamila knelt before her and greedily drank her tears.

The Leaving

"We will have to get rid of the bed," Bimal says.

His wife Sumitra does not answer immediately. They have been close to discussing the subject several times in the last two months. It has hovered on the rim of their consciousness, dangling just beyond the circle of their increasingly testy conversations about what would be the last big change of their lives. They have decided to sell their house. It is too big. They cannot manage it anymore. With servants hard to come by, even daily maintenance has become tough. Often, there is no one to sweep the driveway. The leaves shed by the neem, mango and jackfruit trees murmur and swirl in the dust. The ground floor remains permanently shut now. Soot clings to the curlicues of the ornamental grilles on the stairway banisters. In the hall upstairs, the vast velvet sofas and tasselled pouffes are covered with dust sheets. The antique chairs are derelict. They haven't been repaired and polished in years. Besides, the house shows its age. It springs new leaks and cracks every day. The plaster falls off here and there, and the walls look bleached and scabbed. When a storm comes or the rain blows hard, the windows have to be tied to the grille with bits of string to keep them from slamming– the fasteners are out of whack and won't slip into their slots anymore. Many of the glass panes have slid off their frames and crashed down. The stuff that held them in place is all shrunk and brittle. Bimal has got some window panes replaced, and some have been simply boarded up. There is a slow hollowing out, a creeping sense of corrosion and decay about the house now that leaves Bimal and Sumitra dazed. And the house feels its sickness too. It rattles and creaks, beseeching its occupants to look to its spreading malaise.

Bimal and Sumitra do their best. Every spring, they call old Faridul, the mason, to stop the rot and stall the crumble.

"What kind of work do you do that the leaks come back bigger every year?" Sumitra demands.

Faridul cackles, laughing through his hennaed beard and rotten bidi-stained teeth.

"This house is too old, Ma. How much can I do? Go on, call the fancy construction people—they will slit your throat with their fancy prices. See if they do any better!"

They don't call the professional roof repair and renovation companies, of course. Bimal has gone through that exercise already. Some years ago he studied the internet for hours and drew up a list of such outfits. Glib, sharp-eyed men who treated the old couple with contemptuous deference came over and studied the house. When they gave their estimates of the costs of the repairs, Bimal winced and quietly shelved the plan. So they go back to Faridul every year and the old man and his grandson do what they can to hold the house together against the coming rains. The house stands like a wounded sentinel, a bleeding hulk of weary pride.

When their children come home for their short annual visits, Bimal and Sumitra raise the subject of the repairs. Their son stays in the US, their daughter in Mumbai. They come with their families and the laughter of children rings through the house, quickening the shuttered rooms with the smell of life. Sumitra takes out the bottles of preserves she made last spring and summer. *Kuler achaar* and *aamer morobba*. The children love it. She makes *koraishutir kochuri* and the children stuff them into their mouths with their small grubby hands. "My *puri* is greee-nah," they shout, dancing around the mahogany table that Sumitra's father-in-law had bought when he became the mayor of Calcutta.

Their son and daughter are not in favour of spending a lot of money to repair the house. "I kind of like its ruinous appeal," says their son, who wears a thoughtful air and teaches comparative literature at Purdue University in Lafayette, Indiana. Their daughter, a brisk and efficient woman, says, "What is the guarantee that after spending so much money, the seepage will stop? What's the guarantee that one year down the line you won't be back to square one?"

"It's not just the seepage from the roof," Bimal says. "Have you seen the outside? The walls? We have to carry out extensive repairs. The house hasn't been painted in 14 years."

His daughter doesn't beat around the bush. "But can you afford this huge expense? I know you want us to help out, Baba, but we really can't. We have a growing family. Our finances are always tight."

Her husband nods his bullet head in agreement.

So Bimal and Sumitra start talking about selling the house. At first it is an impossible kernel of thought. Then slowly, they accept its possibility, and finally, its inevitability. There is no other way, they sigh and tell themselves again and again. It's got to be done. The house is a white elephant, Bimal says. His pension and savings are not enough for its upkeep anymore. Many of their friends and relatives have also sold their ancestral homes to builders. Selling is the last refuge of Calcutta's genteel Bengalis, ceding privilege of location part of their slow scuttle into the margins.

Their children are shocked when they tell them about their decision. They are even more shaken when they hear that Bimal has decided not to accept the builder's offer of two flats in the high-rise that will come up in place of the old house.

"Are you crazy," splutters his daughter. "You want to totally move away? "And where will you go? Baishnabghata? Patuli? You'll leave this Elgin Road house and move into a poky flat in some downmarket area? Come on, Baba, you can't do this–we ought to have a say in the matter too," she exclaims. "You should have taken the two flats!" Her fury fills the room like a stench. She turns to her husband as if to tell him, knock some sense into the head of my obstinate father. But her husband, who is a fund manager, knows a lost cause when he sees one. He says nothing and studies his phone's screen like the balance sheet of a company he is about to invest in.

"I don't know if it's a good idea," their son says coldly, speaking over the phone from the US. "It's our ancestral house after all. We grew up there. It's our roots, our home. It's one thing to unlock the value of the house and develop it. In fact, it's probably the right thing to do now. But why won't you take the flats? I know legally the house belongs to you and you alone, and you can do as you please. But it's also our inheritance. I think you should have taken our views into account instead of presenting us with this fait accompli."

Bimal listens to his son and then replies in his thin dry voice: "As you rightly point out, this is my house and my decision. I refuse to live like a nobody in what was once my own property. Live here along with a 100 other people in a place that belonged to us? No, thank you. I'd much rather take more money and move away."

After he hangs up, he turns to Sumitra and says, "They're livid because they were waiting for us to die so *they* could sell this prime piece of real estate and divide the money between them. Or at least have two flats between them. Well, that's not happening now," he says with satisfaction.

Sumitra rebukes him: "You always think the worst about your children! They are right! It is their inheritance too! Besides, what about us? We could have at least come back here after the new house was built. I would have liked that much better. To let go of...of..." Her voice breaks and she makes a gesture with her arm as though she were about to sweep everything up and draw them close. She looks at her husband of 42 years. His slight stoop. His furrowed brow. His head of sparse white hair. The set of his jaws when his sense of duty and affection towards his family gives way to that hurtful crustiness. Her eyes brim over. These days she often feels as if she were in the midst of a car crash in slow motion. There is a smashing and shattering going on all around her over which she has no control.

"We have gone over this a thousand times, Sumitra," Bimal says, trying to look patient. "We are letting go of everything in any case. Don't start all over again now."

After the sale agreement is signed with the builder, they start looking for a flat. The one they choose in Southend Park—with needless haste, in Sumitra's opinion—is a compromise on a hundred fronts. She doesn't like its smallish rooms, nor the verandah which overlooks another one opposite their house. "No privacy," she says, looking miserably at the rows of wash on the balcony in front.

"Why do we need privacy? Are we newly married," Bimal jokes.

But their mood does not lighten.

They know they will have to sell most of the furniture. The new flat is too small to hold them. They ask their children if they want to keep anything–the massive teak wardrobes, the set of Lazarus chairs, or maybe the antique hat rack that stands on the landing like a creature preserved in amber. Their son mentions the two Jamini Roy paintings that hang in the living room. So does their daughter. "We don't have space for any of the furniture," she says over the phone. "But I could take the two Jamini Roys. And Dida's silver bowls you used to serve *payesh* in."

"Oh, I think we can find space for the paintings in the new house," Sumitra tells her. "Besides, your brother should get one of those too. The silver bowls...I suppose you may as well take them. We haven't used them in years. At least you will be able to put them to some use."

Bimal contacts a shop that deals in second-hand stuff. It is decided that the bulk of the furniture and three generations' worth of accumulated paraphernalia are to go there. And then, when it can't be put off any longer, he broaches the subject of the bed.

It is their bed, the one on which they have slept for 42 years. Sumitra's father-in-law had got it custom-made at great expense when their marriage was fixed. Though it wasn't ready by the time they got married, the bed created a sensation when it arrived nearly a month later. Their relatives landed up to see it. Looks like Queen Victoria's bed, a gawping poor cousin had remarked. Sumitra's father-in-law guffawed whenever he harked back to the incident of the stupefied cousin and her wonder-struck words. He was a large man, not slight like Bimal, and he was given to making a big impact with whatever he said or did. And the bed was all about impact—a great, king-size, four-poster, Burma teak affair with a richly carved headboard shaped like a crown. It had curved animal legs, beginning with tiger faces and ending with fierce tiger paws. It was neither aesthetic nor elegant. Still, Sumitra had been thrilled when it was fitted up in her bedroom. It was unlike anything she had seen before. She loved its ornate grandeur, its over-the-top appeal. To her it epitomised the power and eminence of the house she had married into.

Sumitra and Bimal had lain on its six-inch mattress covered with immaculate snow-white sheets. Every night she would smooth away the creases and tuck in the bed sheet tight before her husband came to her. On some nights she wove a jasmine garland into the coiled rope of her plait. Or wore jewelled pins that winked like an invitation. Her sindoor scintillant in the parting of her jet black hair, she sat on the bed dressed in a pretty saree, hugging her knees and listening to her heart thudding loudly in her ears. The bed waited with her. It was witness to their hesitant intimacy and then their delight in each other. Later, it cradled her firstborn, her beloved son. She would lift him from his crib and place him on the bed, between herself and Bimal, so she could thrill to his sweet, milky proximity. Even today, just standing by the bed, Sumitra can visualise her baby lying there, his tiny fists and perfect little toes, his pearly nails, his exuberant smile, the liquid pools of his eyes...

Was there a time when she was not part of the bed and the bed was not part of her? Sumitra barely remembers. She possesses it as much as it possesses her. Her memories of youth and moments of simple joy have settled into it, poured into its every curve and grain of wood, her passing years distilled and spread across its wide tableland. If she stopped to think about it, she would have said that it was the one constant in her life as things changed about her. Her in-laws' death. Her children growing up. Her greying hair and mottled skin, her slender frame swelling into corpulence. The Studebaker and the Chevrolet in the garage giving way to a Standard Herald and much later, a Maruti 800. Bimal stiffening and souring into the aspect of a man who will never be as successful as his father.... The years went faster and faster, spinning forward with vicious haste and making people and things change, dwindle or disappear. The bed was the only exception. It is as it was. Solid and enduring. It is at once a majestic relic and a repository of Sumitra's past.

And she has been careful to preserve it too. She doesn't let the slightest whiff of decay get to it. She dusts it every day with her bright feather duster, caressing the clefts and crenellations on its carved tiger faces and its florid headboard. She gets it polished every other year. Its every nick and scuff is sanded down, smoothed and shined until the bed glows again. It's the only piece of furniture in their house that is untouched by time. "Burn me with my bed after I die", Sumitra used to joke once. "Not a bad idea," Bimal would deadpan. "It would save the cost of the wood at least."

Naturally, she means to take the bed to their new flat. She does not tell Bimal this, correctly guessing that he would oppose the plan at once. The master bedroom in the new flat is no more than twelve feet by eleven. She has done the math and decided that there would be room enough for the bed. Just about. They would certainly be able to walk around it. It would be a bit cramped, yes, but she cannot be expected to give up all that she holds dear.

And then Bimal declares, "We will have to get rid of the bed."

The quarrel that both of them had anticipated and skirted around, bursts open now. Sumitra is a pliant woman, and willingly or unwillingly, agrees with most of her husband's decisions. But she sticks to her guns on this one. Both of them have their ammunition ready and they face each other and fire away.

"One must be practical," starts Bimal.

"What about my sentiment? How about respecting it for a change?"

"That monstrosity will fill up the entire room! It's a flat, Sumitra, the rooms are like cubby holes–it will look incongruous!"

"Let it, I don't care. You can sleep in another room if you don't like it. And why are we moving into a flat where the rooms are like cubby holes? We could have afforded a bigger and better place with all that money you are getting."

Bimal changes tack: "You think any carpenter will be able to take it apart and then put it back together? After 42 years?"

"We won't know until we try," Sumitra retorts curtly.

"I can't understand this silly attachment you have. It's just a bed, for god's sake!"

Sumitra gives him a hostile stare.

They carry on like this for the next few days. Sometimes they give it a rest and come back to it the next morning or evening. They are like allies who have suddenly unearthed a hidden seam of enmity. And they mine it every day, almost glad to have found something on which they can hang their anger and frustration at the upheaval they have let loose upon their lives.

In these last days before the sale of the house, there is not a minute to spare. They have to go through everything and decide what to keep and what to discard. It's not just the furniture. There are books and utensils, pictures and figurines; there are multiple sets of fine bone china crockery, crystals, porcelain and countless bric-a-brac; there are the clothes they have not worn in years–Sumitra's butter-soft Banarasi silks and Bimal's suits and jackets that come out only for their annual airing before Durga Puja. They tackle one almirah at a time and sort through the stuff. Bimal wants to speed up, while Sumitra picks up everything and looks carefully. Each little object sparks a rainbow rush of memories, making her want to pause and rewind. But Bimal becomes impatient and tells her to hurry up. It makes Sumitra madder, her grief sharper. Does he not feel anything? Is no memory sacred to him? She doesn't recognise this man who is her husband. When did he become so indifferent? When did he become this desiccated old man? She sits amidst the debris of years, alone in her desperate caring and the certitude of her loss. At times they remember their unresolved spat over the bed and start to argue once again. By now it is clear that Sumitra will have her way on this one. It is also clear that Bimal will fight it to the end.

"We haven't even opened the box room," Sumitra says, holding on to a chair and hauling herself up from the floor. She is overcome with fatigue and her arthritis is worse. Her feet and knees are stiff from sitting on a low stool for hours. She looks at the mound of stuff they are to throw or give away. She wants to flop down on the floor and cry. Instead, she steels herself and hobbles towards the next cabinet.

Their daughter lands up a few days before they are to move out. She has come to take the silver bowls promised to her, and maybe her grandmother's exquisite brass *pancha pradeep*—if it can be found. The *pradeep* has not been seen for years.

"This is so awful," she says looking around.

"Yes, it is. But don't start ticking off your father," Sumitra says. "He doesn't express things much, but I know his heart is also breaking."

"Well, I'm not so sure, Ma. You've always stuck up for him shamelessly."

Sumitra smiles. She is glad her brusque and acquisitive daughter is here. "Why don't you keep Dadu's Chinese lacquer cabinet," she says. "And the hexagonal marble table too. They are such beauties and not bulky either. Will fit in nicely in your Bombay flat."

"What I'd really love to have is the Queen Anne chair. Remember how I used to call it 'quinine' chair?"

Mother and daughter laugh together.

"Take, *na*," Sumitra says. "I'd be happy if you did. It will be as good as new if you get it repaired, polished and re-upholstered."

"Let's see the silver and brass stuff first," her daughter says.

They go into the box room where all the brass and silver are stored along with masses of other things. The dust lies undisturbed here. The air is dank and thick with the smell of mould. It has been several years since anyone has entered this room. Sumitra switches on the light and the hodgepodge of dusty trunks, suitcases, boxes and odds and ends swims into view. The forgotten refuse of years. The things the household jettisoned, but didn't get around to throwing away.

"I can't remember when I last came inside this room," Sumitra's daughter says. "Gosh, how are we ever going to find anything here?"

"Don't worry, I know which trunk has the brass and silver," her mother says.

They open the trunk and take out the utensils—heavy bronze plates, bowls and glasses that are black with tarnish and laced with verdigris. There is a big brass bell, and a lot of copper *pujor bashon* too—vessels meant for pujas. They go through the silverware and Sumitra's tired face lights up when she finds a set of utensils engraved with her and Bimal's names. She holds up a silver plate and says, "Your grandma served me rice in this on the day of my *bhaat-kapor*—when the bride officially becomes a part of the house. These were bought for Baba and me when we got married."

"You should keep them. Don't let Baba sell off everything," says her daughter, keeping aside the silver bowls she wanted and some other silverware, including her grandmother's silver *paan* box and nut cracker. "These can be nice decor items," she says.

They open a few more boxes. All sorts of things spill out—school books, report cards, dolls' dresses, a pair of Japanese fans, woollens Sumitra had knitted for her children when they were small...

Her daughter wrinkles her nose in distaste, "Why on earth did you keep all this junk?"

"I'll go have a bath—I'm all dirty and sweaty," she says a little later and carries out her silver booty.

Sumitra remains sitting on the stool. Her neck and shoulders ache and her mouth is gritty with dust. But she says to herself that she may as well go through all the boxes now. Many of them are from her in-laws' time. She feels she must dig into the past one last time for their sake—her father-in-law who was so extravagant in his affections, her mother-in-law who loved her like a daughter. She must leaf through these remnants of their lives, open these caskets of their memories, before the house they built is demolished and turned to rubble.

So she calls the young maid, and together, they start opening the rest of the boxes. After a quick look, things are put back in. Tomorrow the *kabadiwala* will come and clear out everything. She comes upon a collection of her father-in-law's tobacco pipes. In one box, she finds her mother-in-law's book of recipes written in her own hand. The writing is faded, almost illegible. Still, Sumitra puts it aside. In another box, she discovers some of Bimal's stuff.

A bunch of long playing records from the 1960s. Joan Baez and Dusty Springfield. Elvis Presley and The Beatles. Some dog-eared college books. A copy of *The Rise and Fall of the Roman Empire* and Dale Carnegie's *How To Win Friends and Influence People*. She wonders if her husband would like to keep any of these for the sake of sentiment. She decides that he would not.

Then she spots a black leather-bound notebook sandwiched between a sheaf of *National Geographic* magazines. She recognises it instantly. Bimal used to write in this notebook. He wrote mostly when he was alone. Then he would lock the notebook away in the drawer of his desk. Everyone teased him about it and said that he was a closet poet, scribbling poems in secret. After they got married, Sumitra asked him many times to read his poems to her. There are no poems, her young husband told her shortly. Just some musings, he said. She holds the notebook in her hand. She had forgotten about it completely and cannot recall when Bimal stopped writing in it, or when it disappeared. Her children, her growing responsibilities in the household, are all she remembers from that time. She fingers its cracked leather cover and riffles through its brittle, blotchy yellow pages. Bimal's name is written on the fly leaf in his flowing cursive. She smiles a little. Won't he be surprised when she tells him what she has found?

"O Maima, hurry up, *na*" the maid whines. "So many boxes left still."

"You go finish the dishes and come back," Sumitra tells her. She has begun to read a bit of the notebook. She struggles without her glasses and it's dim under the lick of light that burns in the naked tungsten bulb. But slowly, her eyes formulate the words. The poems are indeed there as everyone had suspected. About a stormy night. About the unjust rich and the toiling poor. About a woman with mysterious eyes...

Good that he never showed them to anybody, Sumitra thinks and grins.

She skips several pages and reads some more. She recognises herself in his words now. Herself and another she does not recognise. One she did not know existed. There are pages and pages of it. The love and the longing. The vexation and the sufferance. Over months, stretching into years. She reads, and slowly, a sense of dreamy calm steals over her, as if she were dead and looking at her own body from somewhere up above. The stuffy little room and its cargo of mildewed memories seem to disintegrate. Noises recede. All she hears is the scratch of Bimal's fountain pen transferring his thoughts on to paper all those years ago. She listens to it scratching on the skin of her soul.

The maid comes back. And Sumitra gently shuts the notebook and puts it back inside the box in which it has lain for decades.

Their daughter leaves for Mumbai early next morning. Bimal and Sumitra drink their tea and wait for the men who are to carry the furniture away. They come and fall to their work, making an awful to-do as they haul the large pieces down the staircase. The air shudders with their cries and shifts and grinds like a tectonic wrench. It takes a long time for the men to carry everything down. Sumitra and Bimal stand by and listen to the emptying rooms echo like an arena where a concert has ended. Soon, the floors are bare except for the black marks outlining the spaces where the furniture stood for so many years. Here a solid rectangle, there four round stains like the pug marks of a beast that's skulked away. Sumitra finds it impossible to focus on the blank spaces, the sudden holes in the beating heart of her existence. She turns away from them, and feeling slightly dizzy, makes her way into the balcony.

They should have sent away the tiger-legged bed too, she thinks as she watches the men heave the furniture into the vehicles. Bimal is right—the bed is too big, and, really, it would look awful in that small room. In a way, it would be a relief to be free of this burden that she has been dusting and polishing for 42 years. What a terrible waste of time it has been, come to think of it. She wants to call Bimal and tell him that she has changed her mind about the bed.

But she does not call him. She remains standing in the balcony long after the lorries have growled away. Sunlight slants into the netted green of the neem, mango and jackfruit trees. She grows drowsy standing there in the unsullied morning light and wonders if the demolition men will spare the trees.

Possessed

The girl was nervous. He could see that. She kept pulling in her upper lip and lowering her eyes as if she expected something dreadful to happen any moment. It made her young face seem younger, like that of a frightened child. She was not particularly pretty. But she had a softness to her that hadn't come through in the pictures. Soft round eyes. A soft fleshy mouth. Hair shiny and soft and hanging about her shoulders in gentle waves. The backs of her hands smooth, satiny and unmarked by veins. The hands of a baby, thought Prof. Sinha. When he walked up to her at Nehru Place metro station, he was struck by how lost she looked. She had come a long way to meet him–all the way from Shahdara. She had told him that she would be wearing a pair of blue jeans and an orange top, and he spotted her at once–bright as a popsicle amidst the drab swell of crowds. The thin strap of her black sequinned cloth bag lay diagonally between her small breasts, pushing them out against the cheap synthetic material of her top. Oh my, Prof. Sinha said to himself, as he approached her with a slow, reassuring smile.

He led her into an eatery amidst the warren of subterranean restaurants that hugged the metro station. The food court would not do, he had decided earlier. It was too noisy and harshly lit. A cool, shaded place with good food and soft music was what was needed to put her at ease. He noticed that she was sweating in spite of the air-conditioning. Her upper lip and forehead were pearled with perspiration. She sat tensely at the edge of the deep upholstered seat, twisting the white napkin with her fingers. Her nails were painted a torrid blue. And the sleeves of her tangerine top were scooped away in the current fashion to reveal the gleaming lozenges of her shoulders. Prof. Sinha tried to look away and asked her what she would like to have.

"A hamburger and a Coca Cola," she said promptly.

She was 15. At least, that's what she had told him when they got chatting all those weeks ago. He saw no reason to disbelieve her. She, on the other hand, was probably wondering how old *he* really was. She had looked surprised when he introduced himself to her at the metro station. He had told her that he was 28, but now that she had seen him in person, he was sure that she thought him older. While he was a trim, well-preserved 46, he knew that no one would mistake him for a 28-year-old. Naturally, he had had to lie about this as about many other things. When he created his fake Facebook profile almost a year ago, he gifted himself a fetching new identity. Ashok Mathur, self-employed, was young and light-hearted. He posted amusing stories and wacky videos and memes. He knew all about the latest movies and music and posted witty comments about them, comments which he often stole from elsewhere. In fact, whenever he had a little time, Prof. Sinha scoured the internet for material to finesse his new persona. He played to the interests of the young. In the early days he used to be a bit embarrassed about the vulgar mishmash of the stuff he put out there. He was, after all, a man of refined taste. He had read English and Classics at Cambridge and considered himself highbrow. And though he was now a part-time lecturer of English at a rundown management institute in Noida, he had the full-time instincts of a fastidious intellectual who was as contemptuous of cat videos as he was of the latest on Kareena Kapoor.

Still, he worked hard on his virtual identity. If he were to succeed, perfection was called for. Happily, perfection was achieved before long. Young women, many of them school girls, began to accept Ashok Mathur's 'friend' requests because he seemed to be such good fun. When he got chatting with some of them on Messenger, they told him they found his profile picture cute. It was a black and white photograph of himself taken by his father when he was three years old, one where he was holding a toy plane and laughing. His wife or his son might have recognised the picture from an ancient family album, but it was unlikely that they would stumble upon it online. His wife had no time for social media and his son had declared that he had moved on to way cooler stuff than Facebook. In fact, no one who knew Aloke Sinha could have connected him to the happy-go-lucky Ashok Mathur who had quickly secured a large number of 'friends' and got a cascade of 'likes' on whatever he posted.

The only snag was that most of the girls wanted to see his recent pictures. Well, they would have to meet him to know what he really looked like, he joked in response. "Mayb u r 2 ugly," some said, shooting off a double row of big grins, winks and smileys. "Oops, you got me there," he bantered. "Actually, I look like the big bad wolf, with big teeth and bad breath," he said and added two tears-of-joy emojis because it was such a grand joke. Sometimes he got serious and told them a bit about himself. The beauty of it was that he could tell them anything across the enabling glow of his computer or smartphone screen. Getting naughty with young girls late in the night, Prof. Sinha, the self-invented internet playboy, spun his web and went on a blithe romp. What a fabulous thing modern technology was, he marvelled. How powerful and liberating. It could tear down regimes and set people free. Just as it had set him free. It had rescued a part of himself that had been smothered under the sorry driftwood of his life.

And so here he was with this girl now, meeting her for the first time.

"I have a confession to make," Prof. Sinha said to her with his most charming smile.

The girl, whose name was Payal, was bent over the menu and was trying to decide between a Juicy Lucy burger and a braised tenderloin burger with caramelised onion and horseradish sauce. She looked up and Prof. Sinha continued. "I am not really 28, you know," he said. "I am 32. But you were so young, so pretty, that I was embarrassed to tell you that I was so much older than you."

At this she tilted her head, looked at him sideways from beneath her short, thick lashes, and gave him a coy, slightly coquettish smile. "I'll take this one–Juicy Lucy," she said and sat up straight. Immediately, his eyes flew to the points of her unripe breasts and he felt a flickering in his groin and a fever in his blood that turned his ears hot. His hand shook when he poured the Coke into her glass and he spilled a bit of the fizzy liquid which the girl quickly mopped up with her napkin.

Well, at least she had lost her nervousness, he thought. It had taken him weeks of careful flattery and flirtation to get her here today. He had drawn her out little by little. She had told him that she studied in Class IX in an English medium school in Shahdara and that she had a younger sister who studied in Class IV. It was clear that she came from a middle class family, where money was always tight. She was angry with her parents because they had not allowed her to go on a class excursion to Nainital last summer. She wanted to take dance lessons after school, but they'd vetoed that proposal too. Prof. Sinha sympathised with her. He told her that a pretty young thing like her deserved all the good things of life. He told her that he had had a tough childhood as well, and that his widowed mother never had the money to buy him even the odd ice cream. That sounded pretty corny to him, but the girl seemed to swallow the story. So he went ahead and said that he would help her with the fees because he had made money now. After all, he was her friend, he typed, and grinned at her naivety. They chatted on Facebook Messenger for days before the conversation turned romantic, and then, sexual.

But gently, gently, now, he had cautioned himself. He didn't want to come on too strong and scare her off. Or worse, have her spread the word around the honeycomb of their online friendships. It was so easy to be misunderstood! No, he would take it slow and nurture this one. She had long-term potential. And really, she was quite perfect, this girl—well-spoken and docile. He had asked her for a picture of herself. Hold the phone like this, and take it, he had instructed her. It took just a few nights' persuasion before she relented. When it popped up in the inbox of his bogus mail ID, he stared at it transfixed. It was her. In the bud. His rosy prize. His little nocturne.

In short, this girl was not a bit like the last one. What an absolute zombie that one was, he recalled with irritation. He had tried to animate her at their first meeting—he'd even promised her an iPhone. Her 14-year-old eyes had lit up for a few seconds before settling back into their blank, catatonic stare. After that first encounter, the girl stopped responding to his messages. He spent several anxious days and nights wondering if she would tattle. But there was no blowback and the girl all but vanished from his news feed. And crouching behind his unblemished three-year-old self, Prof. Sinha had continued to spread his virtual charm, chatting with a few likely young friends and testing and probing to see if he could harvest them for his delicious game.

The girl called Payal was prattling cheerfully now. Munching on a burger that nearly hid her face, she told him that Shahdara to Nehru Place was the longest metro ride she had ever taken (prompting him to reimburse the 40-rupee fare at once). She talked at length about her ambition of becoming an air hostess, even though her parents were dead against the idea. "They want me to become a doctor or a CA," she said. "They want me to go on studying my whole life, *kya?*" she exclaimed. She turned her big soft eyes on Prof. Sinha and asked him if he would help her.

"You know I will, Payal," he told her. Smooth, kind and gallant, his hot gaze licking her child-woman face, Prof Sinha reached for her hand across the table and promised her eternal support.

After some time he got up and sat next to her. When he edged closer, she did not move away. He put his hand on her back a few times. He was itching to touch her more urgently now. Oh, to possess this nubile Proserpina! To stroke this innocent, untouched thing! Cup her snug adolescent rump and run his tongue up her bony spine, around her pristine neck, and the whorled shell of her ear! He brought his face close to hers and inhaled her infant scent of talcum powder while his mind twitched and throbbed, picturing the next time.

Getting off at Green Park metro station, Prof. Sinha began to walk towards his house. He was still savouring his meeting with the girl and smiling to himself that it had gone so well. The long August twilight was spilling into evening now and the traffic breasted it like a slow-moving sea. He walked carefully as part of the road was dug up into a trench in the service of some deep civic good. Gusts of red dust flew from it as cars ground past. Prof Sinha forgot to grimace–such was his jubilant mood.

Once he reached home, he hid his joy as though it were something he had stolen. He didn't want his wife Beena to sniff out his excitement. Beena was a tall, thin and energetic woman. She too was an academic, but unlike him, her career had gone exceedingly well. She was now the head of the department of economics at a top college in Delhi where she preferred to be addressed as 'Dr Sinha' rather than as a mere 'Professor'. She commanded the respect of her students and peers, had published several authoritative studies on the complexities of labour participation in the workforce, and was tipped to be principal of her college in the not too distant future. She had inherited their house in Green Park from her father and, on the whole, was fairly satisfied with herself and what she had achieved. Prof. Sinha went slightly in fear of her, even though he admired her brilliance. Indeed, his own intellectual arrogance was nothing compared to that of his wife. Her success had weaponised it, and he was never more aware of his inadequacies than when he was in the presence of its fierce, blowtorch glare. On her part, Beena treated him with impatience. He had been a disappointment to her. He had not lived up to his potential. With his Cambridge degree he could have gone on to have a decent, if not an exceptional, career. But he had frittered it away. One telling look from her could remind him of all this and more.

"There you are," Beena said in her slightly braying voice. "I wondered where you had got to. Your phone rang out."

"Oh, I was attending a seminar and then forgot to unmute the phone," Prof. Sinha replied, trying to sound offhand. "Why, what's the matter?"

Beena looked at her husband. Her big shell-rimmed spectacles flashed as if to warn him about lying to her. She was about to say, "What seminar? And where?", but she changed her mind and said instead, "Abhi's got into a scrape again. It seems he slipped out of school at lunchtime yesterday and went to watch a movie with some friends. The principal called me. According to him, Abhi was the ring leader."

"Really?" Professor Sinha laughed aloud. "Well, at least he is sharpening his leadership skills."

Beena tightened her mouth. Then she sternly ticked him off for not taking the matter seriously, reminded him that their 17-year-old son was going to sit for his Class XII exams next year, and instructed him to have a talk with the boy. "He needs to shape up," she said. "I am reconciled to the fact that he won't be sitting for the engineering or medical entrance exams. Because he won't get through them anyway. But at this rate he won't get into a decent college even if he wants to study history! I'd rather you did the talking for a change. Maybe I intimidate him. I don't know. Really, I have no idea how Abhi got to be so feckless," she said, making it clear from her tone that she actually had a very good idea.

Abashed, Prof. Sinha agreed to have a man-to-man chat with his son. It was not something he looked forward to, since he knew that the boy treated him with barely disguised contempt. Besides, he too did not much care for his son. He had felt a mild hostility towards Abhi ever since he reached puberty. On top of that, he had shot up in the last year or so, and was now a head taller than his father. Prof. Sinha knew that he was supposed to feel proud about this—he had heard other parents brag about their offspring growing taller than themselves—but truth was, he found it irritating that Abhi could literally look down upon him.

He knocked and entered his son's room. Abhi was sitting at his desk with industrial-sized headphones clapped around his ears. When he saw his father he took them off. "I didn't hear you knock," he remarked with disapproval. He had become very vocal about his need for privacy lately.

Prof. Sinha pointed to his headphones.

"Ah, right, sorry," Abhi said laconically.

The boy looks dopey, Prof. Sinha thought with distaste. But he assumed a friendly tone and asked, "So how're things? How's school? Your Mum was saying you're in a spot of trouble?"

Abhi, all greasy hair and gangly grasshopper limbs, slid deeper into his chair. A football lay at his feet. He shifted it around with his foot and said, "Oh, it's no big deal. It was, like, you know, a dare. And c'mon, we're almost in college! Anyway, we've been given a warning and let off. So tell Mom to chill."

"I'm relieved," said his father. "So which movie did you see?"

"*Kingsman.*"

"Any good?"

"Oh, Awsm!"

Prof. Sinha let out a mental sigh and wondered why the word 'awesome' had such an odd effect on him. He had embraced the word online, and like his virtual friends, used it to express approval, delight, ecstasy and a range of other happy emotions. It was the verbal equivalent of an emoticon, and in his Ashok Mathur persona, he loved its clipped economy, its multi-tasking élan. And yet, strangely, his hackles rose whenever the word reared at him offline. He considered his son—this alien creature who preferred the English Premier League to Indian cricket. Abhi's vocabulary consisted almost entirely of words like "wow", "awesome" and "cool". But none seemed as loathsome as "awesome". When Abhi or any of his students uttered the word, it sounded like a pre-historic grunt, a sort of a brutish proto word, whose very multi-functionality was an assault on his linguistic sensibilities. Really, I ought to think this thing through sometime, Prof. Sinha pondered seriously. The dialectical opposition between my online and offline selves could make for an interesting study.

When he retreated into his bedroom at night, Prof. Sinha shut the door and locked it. His family knew that he stayed up late every night to work on his book, which was tentatively titled, 'Idolatry and the Idea of India'. In reality, he hadn't worked on it for nearly two years and it revolted him to even look at his confused and fragmented research. He suspected that Beena knew that he had abandoned the book project, but if she was happy to keep up the pretence, so was he.

He logged into his computer to see if the girl called Payal was online. She was not. But he didn't worry about it. They had made a connection today. A real connection. He would send her a passionate message. He would press the advantage now and reel her in.

He took off his shirt and looked at himself in the mirror. He noted his greying chest hair. His too thin arms. His slim, aristocratic hands. His muscles beginning to yield to the tug of gravity. Still, his stomach was almost flat. Almost. What a pity the hair on his chest couldn't be dyed satisfactorily. Maybe he should shave it off? His eyes glittered back at him from the mirror. He felt a curious energy today. There was a lifting and surging inside him that made him feel airborne.

He had given the girl a gift this afternoon. A make-up box with a set of eye-shadows and blush. Pleased, she had flashed him a big smile.

"You'll tell me if you need anything, hmm?"

She nodded shyly. And he warmed himself in the light of her trust and congratulated himself on his luck.

He would have to be careful, of course. It was not just about keeping the girl hooked. There was also Beena to think of. After that unpleasant incident at the college seven years ago, she had told him that she would throw him out of the house if there was ever a whiff of a scandal again. Three of his students had complained against him. Silly, vicious creatures. He had done nothing to them. Nothing substantive, that is. But they went after him. First, one of them complained. Then two more. It was a nightmare. Quite, quite surreal. There was an enquiry, but frankly, he never had a chance. Those idiots with long faces had made up their minds about him right from the start. He was forced to resign and the city's academic fraternity, who obviously had nothing better to do, feasted on the story for months. He had been sacked for inappropriate behaviour, they said. 'Predator' was the word that was used, he believed. What a laugh! If that were predatory, he had to say they didn't know the first thing about it. They didn't know what he could do. What he had done in the past.

But this time he was truly in a fix. It took him three years to find another job. And when he did, it was at a third-rate management institute where he was supposed to impart English skills to future managers. A completely futile exercise, of course, since most of them had a fine disregard for grammar and syntax and conversed confidently in their ghastly English. Did these kids learn nothing at school? It was deplorable, Prof. Sinha fumed. Even so, he clung to his three-days-a-week visiting lecturership. It wasn't much—but it was something.

And he had stayed out of trouble. His workplace could never again be compromised. When the scandal broke seven years ago,

Beena had not spoken to him for a month. He had admitted to her that he had made a fool of himself with only one girl. The other two were a conspiracy, hatched so they could get rid of him. Even one incident was too much, Beena said. She shed a few angry tears and said she had always known that there was something wrong with him, something twisted and sick. "Abhi needs a father," she told him in a hard voice. "But there mustn't be a next time." Then she shifted him into another bedroom and they did not discuss the subject again.

So, yes, he must watch his step. Anonymity is all, thought Prof. Sinha, as he composed his message of love and lust and clicked to send it Payal's way.

Three days later, Prof. Sinha was sitting in the staff room of the management institute where he worked. He shared this room with four other members of the faculty. He was on good terms with his colleagues and often discussed politics and current affairs with them. If they knew about the ancient blot on his career, they did not seem to care. On the contrary, they seemed to enjoy his elegant company and appreciate his knowledge of the arts and letters. That morning they were talking about the downturn in the economy and young Ashwin Govil, who taught business policy and strategic management, said, "I am not so sure, you know. Too early to say that we are going into a serious economic slowdown and we better bite the bullet."

"Not to mention the bullet train," quipped Prof Sinha.

They were laughing when the phone rang. Prof. Govil took the call and gestured to Prof. Sinha. Surprised, he walked over to his colleague's desk. He had never received a call on the institute's land line.

When he said "Hello", a male voice asked,

"Professor Sinha?"

"Yes, this is he," he replied loftily.

"*Saala chutiya,*" the man swore. "Minor *ke saath ashleelta karte ho*, you commit indecent acts with a minor?"

Prof. Sinha froze. His mouth went dry and he heard his heart hammering against his ribs, pounding in his ear, in his throat, his heart almost bursting, as the man spoke and he listened. Through the hurricane of his panic, he wondered dimly if his colleagues could hear the man's hideous words pouring into his skull. He cupped the receiver tighter with his hand to keep that impossible voice down, and not let it go scattering across the room, exposing him, nailing him, making him wriggle and cower. He heard himself saying "yes". And "yes" once again. And again. And again.

They were all watching him. "Bad news," Prof. Govil asked when he replaced the receiver.

"You look ill, Aloke," said another. "Let me get you a glass of water."

He ran his tongue over his numb lips. "No, no, it's all right," he said. "Yes, some bad news. I have to go... Ashwin, will you tell the dean?"

They told him not to worry and to let them know if he needed any help.

"Yes, yes, thanks," he said. "You are all very kind."

Fleeing from the institute in a cab, Prof. Sinha tried to think rationally. He was being blackmailed, his terrified mind screamed back at him. They know about me and Payal! And they know all about me! They know where I live, where I work! The man said he had followed him to his house the day he met the girl at Nehru Place metro station. And, oh my god, this meant the little bitch was in cahoots with the blackmailer! It was a set-up right from the beginning! He had been throughly played! The man had threatened to go to his wife with screen shots of his messages to the girl and photographs of him sitting with her at the restaurant. Photographs of him touching her. The police would easily track down his fake account to his IP address and his computer, the man said. Could they actually do that? Prof. Sinha wasn't sure. But he couldn't take a chance. Beena would definitely believe the story. And the police could haul him up. He could be accused of molesting a child! And god knew what other nonsense they would dream up! As if the girl was a poor young innocent! The little whore! The teenage trickster! He had covered his tracks so well, but now everything had been ripped to shreds. The biter bit. The trapper trapped. He nearly wept in frustration. It was monstrous! He had treated the girl so well! He had almost loved her!

He deleted his fake Facebook account and email address the moment he got home. But he had no idea if that would erase the digital trail left by the man called Ashok Mathur. When the next call came–this time on his mobile phone–Prof. Sinha went to the terrace to take it. The man put a figure to the blackmail now. Ten lakhs or else. Either that or they were going to call his wife and then the police. When he tried to negotiate feebly, the man laughed and said, "*Jail jana hai kya*–want to go to jail?"

Over the next few days he scraped the barrel of his meagre savings and got the money together. He did not sleep and nor could he eat much. I am like a tragic hero, pursued by the Furies, he thought wildly. They're closing in upon me, and I have nowhere to run, no place to hide.

"What's wrong with you?" Beena asked at breakfast one day. "You look terrible!"

"Just a touch under the weather," he told her.

On the appointed evening he drove to a stretch of Dwarka where apartment blocks rose like silent ziggurats with vast deserted spaces in between. Cars whizzed by infrequently, disappearing in pinpoints of red tail lights. Prof. Sinha parked his battered Maruti Swift and got out. He waited next to a rank rubbish tip. He trembled slightly, at once frightened and disgusted. The whole situation was vulgar and cheesy, he thought. It was astounding that he found himself in this mess–that he, Aloke Sinha, was submitting to blackmail by these filthy lowlifes.

Soon, two men approached him. He heard a low voice muttering "Payal!" which was supposed to be the 'codeword'.

Prof. Sinha hurriedly took out the big parcel of cash from his laptop bag. One of the men snatched it from his hands and said, "If this is even one rupee less, you'll hear from us."

"I don't have any more money," Prof. Sinha said with dignity, "So don't bother pestering me again."

At once he felt an explosion in his chest. He collapsed on the pavement and the men melted into the darkness.

More than a year passed. Prof. Sinha did not think too much about that awful incident now. But for a long time afterwards, his memory of being hit and falling on the pavement kept him in a state of constant dread. He had lain there, doubled up in a cloud of unimagined pain. He clung to the ground on all fours and retched. A couple of people walked past, but none came to his aid. After sometime he got up, dragged himself to the car and drove back home. He returned to work a few days later and picked up the usual routine of his life. But his nerves remained on edge. He flinched each time his phone or the doorbell rang. He looked over his shoulders to see if he was being shadowed. He stayed off the internet. He neglected to dye his hair.

The blackmailers did not call again. And bit by bit, his panic ebbed away. Life returned to its old unthreatening ways, and there came a time when Prof. Sinha at last managed to put the experience behind him.

His son was in college now. Beena had been right about Abhi. His Class XII results had been disappointing. He was studying political science in a not-so prestigious institution and she was trying to badger him into preparing for the law entrance exams next year. Prof. Sinha, as was his wont, preferred to keep a judicious distance from his son's affairs.

These days he often went and sat in a neighbourhood park. Sometimes he went for a run around its paved jogging track. The afternoons were pleasant here. He enjoyed watching the children clambering up and down the slides and the jungle gyms. He liked to see them play. Their shouts floated towards him like a medley of birdcall–sharp, sweet and true. He knew most of their faces by now. His favourite was a little girl, about seven or eight, who was in a pink and white polka-dotted pinafore dress today. He saw her going up to the swing. Soon, she was swinging herself high. Higher and higher she went, her short hair aloft and her dress fluttering up. "I want to be an astronau-au-au-ght," she cried as she climbed the sunset air. Prof. Sinha watched her laughing face and her fair plump legs dangling like fruit. A smile came to his lips. And he went home humming a little tune.

When he stepped into the living room, he found Beena sitting with a mug of coffee, marking some papers. He could hear his son playing his keyboards in his room.

"Abhi seems to have got himself a girl friend," she said, looking at him over the rim of her glasses.

"Really?" he said indifferently.

A litter later, Abhi came out with the girl to see her to the door. On the way he paused and said,

"Dad, meet my friend Polly."

"Hello," said the girl called Payal, and smiled.

Saturn's Ring

The meeting between the two families had gone off swimmingly. After the introductions and the polite queries, the ice was broken over tea and snacks. Then Mrs Banerjee and Mrs Lahiri chatted amiably about the difficulty of getting good servants and shared anecdotes about their unbelievable cheek and their untold depredations. Mr Banerjee, who was the head of the legal division of a big multinational company, held forth on the state of the economy and why the country's laws were failing to bring the corrupt to book. He found Mr Lahiri to be an attentive listener with an agreeable habit of saying "exactly!" at regular intervals. It turned out that Mr Lahiri could also tell a good story. He narrated a rather ingenious piece of shenanigan—a crooked deal that he had come across recently in the state's land revenue department, which is where he worked. To which Mr Banerjee, who was a tall, heavily built man with a big belly and a fleshy, sweaty face, shook his head and exclaimed, "I tell you!" in pleasurable outrage. Amidst this general feast of reason and flow of soul, the boy and the girl sat stiffly at opposite ends of an ornately carved sofa. They looked like characters in walk-on parts who had been ordered to hang around for a while. They had tried to converse in short, spasmodic bursts and had then lapsed into an awkward silence.

But that was to be expected. As a concession to modernity they had been encouraged to talk and get to know each other a little at this first meeting. That did not, however, mean that they should start chatting shamelessly. The boy, or rather the young man, was thinnish, with an incipient paunch. Dressed in snuff-coloured trousers and a white and pink checked shirt buttoned at the wrist despite the heat of summer, he sat somewhat inelegantly with his legs wide apart. He was dark, but it wasn't one of those humdrum shades of *moyla rong*–the phrase Bengalis use to describe the not-so-fair, which translates literally to 'dirty colour'. His complexion was a deep, spectacular mahogany and against it, his small, even teeth seemed brilliant white when he smiled. He had a smooth, watchful face that revealed little, and his neatly combed, well-oiled hair gleamed like new-laid tar. A veteran of many a bride-hunt, he eyed the girl with practised surreptitiousness. The girl, Anisha, barely looked at him. She knew she was the one who was being shown–she was the *seen* rather than the seer, the acted upon rather than the actor. So she wore a serene expression on her face, kept her hands folded on her lap in an attitude of humility, and looked nowhere in particular.

Anisha bore these visits with calm fortitude. The thing she hated most about them was that her mother insisted that she dress in a silk saree and some light jewellery. Sarees made her look terribly ungainly, she thought, and jewellery pricked her delicate skin. The whole ritual was like a piece of unpleasant theatre to her. The dressing up, the stock questions, the appraising looks, and the strained chit chat–she loathed it all. Yet it never occurred to her to tell her parents that she would not subject herself to another 'showing'. To her it was something tiresome, like studying for an exam, that had to be gone through for a greater good. Her parents wanted her married and settled now that she was almost

24 years old. And Anisha, who was a docile and dutiful girl, generally fell in with whatever her parents wanted.

When the Lahiris left, Mr and Mrs Banerjee looked at each other.

"Well?" said Mr Banerjee.

"I really liked them," came Mrs Banerjee's prompt and emphatic verdict. She was a small, fair, bird-like woman with shrewd, penetrating eyes and she was used to telling her husband how a person ought or ought not be viewed. "They seemed very down to earth. The boy looked very nice too. Very simple and respectful."

"I agree," said Mr Banerjee, nodding his head. He was relieved that his wife's views matched his own. "Extremely nice people. And Mr Lahiri...a most likeable chap. Of course...he did not seem to be in a very senior position in the land revenue department. But they have a lot of power, these government people."

"That's right. And the boy is a chemical engineer. He has good prospects. Besides, he is the only child–which is a huge plus point. Now if only..." Mrs Banerjee murmured with the wistful air of a mother who has set her sights on a suitable boy for her daughter.

It has to be said that despite the generous praise they heaped on their guests, both Mr and Mrs Banerjee felt that the Lahiris did not quite belong to the same class as theirs. They had both surmised that the latter probably lived more modestly than them, that their car was probably cheaper than theirs, and most importantly, they probably never got invited to–or occasionally threw–such things as cocktail parties. In short, they were quite deficient in many of the attributes that went with being the "proper sort" in the eyes of the Banerjees. Mr Banerjee's ascent up the corporate ladder from a relatively humble background had made them fiercely conscious of their status and both husband and wife tried to live up to its exacting standards with a zealousness that would have put the average social climber to shame. They had decorated their house in what Mrs Banerjee thought was a suitably classy fashion—with lots of heavy, carved (and rather ugly) furniture and a groaning array of anaemic landscape paintings, elaborate statuary, and glassware. They had made sure that their children attended posh schools, took piano lessons and could tell their Mozart from their Strauss. After Mr Banerjee's latest elevation a couple of years ago, Mrs Banerjee had chopped off her long hair in an effort to look the part of a sophisticated, senior vice-president's wife. Dyed an unabashed black, it now hung dull and lifeless about her shoulders and made her look older than she was. She had even tried attending kitty parties with the wives of some of her husband's colleagues. But her style was peremptory and unsubtle and despite her street-smart canniness, she found it tough to match her wits with women who were silken even when they stung.

In other words, Mrs Banerjee knew enough about what she called "high society" to conclude that the Lahiris were not part of it. But that was of no consequence. Not this time. Not when they were desperate to arrange a match for their daughter. Besides, she had found Mrs Lahiri far more simpatico than many of the wives of her husband's colleagues.

And so Mrs Banerjee sighed again and said, "Now god willing...Of course, the boy is a bit dark..."

"He isn't a bit dark, Ma, he's very dark!" Anisha burst out suddenly. She had helped herself to some of the leftover *kochuri* and *aloor dum* and had been polishing them off with concentration. She had not eaten anything in front of the guests as it was not seemly that a shy, would-be bride should display her appetite. Her parents had forgotten that she was in the room—which they were often wont to do.

"And he has a terrible pronunciation," Anisha continued. "He said he wanted a bit more 'soogaar' in his tea! He also said 'sho' when he wanted to say 'so'," she giggled.

"Did he," Mr Banerjee laughed. "Actually, even the father has a funny accent."

But his wife was displeased. "Don't encourage her," she told Mr Banerjee. "And are you such a *memsaab*," she said coldly to her daughter, "that you're looking down on people and their accents? You'd be lucky if they accepted you. He is a very good boy. And stop eating so many potatoes. You'll put on weight."

"I don't want to marry him," Anisha declared quietly and left the room.

Mr and Mrs Banerjee were astounded. They looked at each other in disbelief. They were not accustomed to such defiance from their daughter. She had actually disagreed with what they were saying!

Trying to control her anger, Mrs Banerjee said to her husband, "See how opinionated and temperamental she's getting? The sooner we get her married off the better!"

Anisha stood shaking slightly as she peeled off her silk saree. She took off the jewellery jerkily, as if she could not bear to have them on her body for another moment. They got tangled in her hair and she yanked at them, not caring if she pulled out a few hairs or broke a link in the gold chain. She was not unlike her mother to look at—fair, fine-boned, with small, delicate features and a pointed chin. She had a snub nose, which made her look a bit childish. Indeed, there was a general look of immaturity about her—a sort of wide-eyed unreadiness—that struck one immediately. And much like a child, her chin trembled with emotion now. That horrid black man! That unsmart oaf with the ridiculous accent! One look at him and she had thought her parents would reject him outright. Only good manners and her rigid training in matters such as this had made her sit through the whole thing. And now they were saying they liked him! She was furious with her parents, and a parallel strand of thought went like a television runner in her mind, marvelling at the breaking news of her own fury.

For Anisha was simply not used to being angry with her family. She treated her parents with absolute, unflagging deference. She had never questioned them or their decisions. When she was a child she was quiet and obedient. As a teenager she threw no tantrums and did not evince the slightest desire to be rebellious. Her passage from childhood to teenage to womanhood had been one continuum of placid, imperturbable docility. There had been no false notes, no discordant moods. She poured herself into the mould her parents had set out for her and was perfectly content. She had been a diligent student and always managed to get decent grades, unlike her brother Mihir, who, older to her by two years, barely scraped through school and college. Mihir had now been placed as a management trainee in the same company where Mr Banerjee worked. It was pure nepotism, but naturally, the Banerjees did their best when it came to their son. However, Anisha, who had been keen to study further after graduating from college, wasn't allowed to. Her parents did not want her to get 'over-qualified' lest she lost out on some good match. While Mihir attended evening classes at a mediocre management institute, Anisha, the brainier of the two, had signed up for art lessons because her parents thought an artistic hobby would not be inimical to the profession of wifery on which she was about to be launched.

Anisha did not mind that her brother was the favourite of her parents. On the contrary, because they thought the world of Mihir, she thought so too. She was utterly devoted to him while he treated her with friendly contempt. She did not resent that either. It was all part of the grand design of the Banerjee household, where Anisha had always come last in the pecking order. Even the servants knew that the sorriest pieces of meat or chicken were to be served to her. If she ever stopped to think about it, which she assuredly never did, she would have shrugged and thought that was just the way it was. That was just the way she was fated to be.

In fact, fate occupied a big chunk of Anisha's estimation of herself. To her, fate was not simply a four-letter word. It was a dark, palpable presence that stalked her every move. She could not recall when her parents first told her that she had been born under a malignant confluence of planets that stamped her with no end of ill luck. As far back as she could remember, the knowledge was there like a petrifying weight around her neck, like manacles around her feet, pulling her back and slowing her down. She had been told that her mother had sobbed for days after her baby daughter's horoscope was charted and read out. The baby was a child of Shani or Saturn in all its evil aspects and a Rakshas Gon (mark of the demon) to boot. The astrologers and pandits had declared that though she was not quite so unlucky herself, she could bring destruction to her near and dear ones. That is, unless adequate protection was taken.

You couldn't blame Mr and Mrs Banerjee for not making sure. They went high and low, consulted a battery of fortune tellers, *tantriks* and other such specialists who knew all about the vagaries of the stars. To a man—perhaps there was the odd woman too—they said that the angelic baby girl with a head full of brown ringlets was a toxic piece of goods. Drastic remedial measures were called for.

Mr and Mrs Banerjee took no chances. They acted on expert advice and resorted to every amulet, gem stone and ritual prescribed in astrology, tantra, and old wives' tales to neutralise their daughter's malignant aura. If Anisha wore a turquoise ring so she wouldn't harm her father, Mr Banerjee carried an amulet to protect himself from her. Mihir wore two rings to beef up his astrological defences against his sister. He joked that they were Saturn's rings and teased her cruelly when they were children. Only Mrs Banerjee was apparently blessed with a horoscope that made her immune to her daughter's accursed influence.

Yet it was she who disliked Anisha most. She considered her daughter to be some sort of an evil alien, a she-devil who would wreak havoc on her family given the slightest leeway. What made it worse was that Anisha looked so much like her own self. It was a constant and intolerable reminder that she was her own flesh and blood. If Mrs Banerjee had belonged to more primitive times, she might have abandoned her ill-fated child. Or, who knows, perhaps killed her. She had mentioned this to Mr Banerjee a few times when Anisha was a child—as a purely hypothetical scenario, of course. Besides, there were laws these days.

Since Mrs Banerjee considered herself an educated, enlightened woman, she steeled herself to do her duty. Anisha was an affliction and she had to bear it, and fight it to the best of her ability. She kept her daughter on a tight leash, lest the poison in her awakened and consumed them all. She ticked her off continuously. Her walk, her talk, her conduct, her dress, her friends—everything was rigidly monitored and severely controlled. Mrs Banerjee never stooped so low as to actually blame her daughter for her evil horoscope. But it was an oft-repeated matter of fact, and more than all her mother's bullying strictures, it cowed Anisha into a state of pathological submissiveness. For a girl who was supposed to be endowed with otherworldly powers to do harm, Anisha turned out to be a person with about as much will as a rag doll. She was a triumph of social engineering and Mrs Banerjee often congratulated herself silently that she had been successful in beating her daughter's diabolic traits into shape.

Hence, Anisha's sudden show of defiance regarding the man who had come to see her was both astonishing and unprecedented. Her mother meant to get to the bottom of it, and now she blew into Anisha's room like a hostile wind and demanded to know what on earth was wrong with her.

"Baba and I found your behaviour very strange," she said coldly. "What's got into you?"

Anisha was sitting slouched at her study desk in her blouse and petticoat. The royal blue Kanjeevaram saree lay in a shimmering heap on the bed. The jewellery too lay scattered where she had discarded them. She had an immature figure—flat-chested and narrow-hipped—and in her blouse and petticoat she looked like a child who had had a bad day at a fancy dress party. She was biting her nails assiduously, tearing off half moons of nail and spitting them out. It was one habit in her daughter that Mrs Banerjee had failed to stamp out.

Without looking at her mother, Anisha said woodenly, "I'll never marry that man."

"Aren't you going a little too fast? He may not want to marry you either. Have you forgotten how many have rejected you? One look at your horoscope and people are scared away!"

"Good," Anisha said. "I hope it scares these people too!"

"I must say you are being very foolish. It's too early to argue about all this, but I can't believe you are making up your mind about a person just because he is a little dark."

"He is not a little dark—he is black," Anisha retorted, "You dislike dark people yourself! You always say, oh my god, so and so's so dark! You're always saying you're so glad that Mihir and I have got your complexion." She looked at her mother sideways, shocked at her own daring, shocked that she had raised her voice and said so much. But seeing that Mrs Banerjee was quite speechless at her unbelievable mutiny, she continued, "You don't even allow me to wear black!"

This was true. Anisha was forbidden to wear black because more than one astrologer had told the Banerjees that the colour would make their daughter 'stronger', and hence manifestly more evil. They said that her ruling planet Saturn would get an added incentive to do its worst if she so much as wore a scrap of black on her person. The advice was rigorously followed, and black was banished from pretty much everything Anisha wore or used.

Another girl might have hankered after that which was denied her. But not Anisha. Her mother had indoctrinated her so thoroughly with the "black means bad" mantra, that over time she actually came to abhor the colour. To Anisha, black smelt of terror, and death and nothingness—that which could strip her of the familiar and condemn her to nameless horrors. She disliked dark-skinned people with equal energy—and this bias too had been bred into her. Mrs Banerjee was a skin colour fundamentalist, proud of her own fair complexion and sneering in her contempt for the dark-skinned. The family echoed her smug racism and it was understood chez Banerjee that the dark were ugly and inferior. It was understood, as Anisha pointed out to her mother with such uncharacteristic show of spirit, that they simply were not in the same league. So she was justly bewildered and outraged that the rules had been suddenly turned on their head.

If Mrs Banerjee was nonplussed by her daughter's outburst, it took her only a few moments to recover her composure. She emitted a grim smile and said, "I see that you are becoming quite wilful and belligerent–arguing for the sake of it, bringing up all kinds of irrelevant issues. Once and for all, let me make it clear: If we find a good match for you, someone who is qualified and who has a horoscope to go with yours, you shall be married to him. Whether you like it or not. Dark! Huh! Nobody's ready to have her and she's complaining about someone being too dark! Now put away the jewellery in their cases and bring them to my room. And fold your saree properly and hang it up."

She barked out the last order like a sergeant major to a sloppy private. Then she turned around and strode away, leaving Anisha gnawing her cuticles with hungry abandon.

Anisha did not come out for dinner that night. Mr Banerjee, who was fond of his daughter in spite of his wife, wanted to go and coax her into eating something. But Mrs Banerjee would have none of it.

"Let her be," she said, her mouth set in a thin, implacable line. "The time for indulging her is over. If she doesn't want dinner, so be it."

The next morning Anisha took her place at the breakfast table as usual. Her parents and her brother were already there. The morning sun streaked into the dining room, opening a pathway of light across the yellow and blue printed table cloth. Anisha felt its warmth and noticed how it licked the fruit bowl and picked out the red blush of the apples and the smooth green of the sweet limes and lay bright and translucent on the cluster of pale yellow bananas. The bowl of fruit looked perfect today, like a still life painting, thought Anisha. Then her mother helped herself to an apple and the fruits shifted and rolled, destroying the exquisite harmony of the picture.

Anisha felt quite all right now. She was almost happy–happy to be in this sunlit room with her family, happy to participate in an everyday ritual that spelt comfort and continuity. She had sunk into an uneasy slumber last night, and had got up at two in the morning and devoured a packet of Cream Cracker biscuits. But daylight had dispelled her sense of hurt outrage. The to-do of the previous evening seemed quite unreal and unnecessary now. How could she have forgotten that this match too was bound to fizzle out, just like so many others had in the last couple of years? Her horoscope would come to her rescue, and the dark man with the silly accent would be forgotten forever. She felt ashamed about her behaviour last night and would have apologised for it, but for the fact that that would have meant bringing up the embarrassing episode again.

Then Mihir, who had been out with friends till late in the night and had only just been brought up to speed about the events of last evening, grinned and said, "Hey, An, I hear a certain Mr Coal India came to woo you yesterday!"

"Ha, ha, very funny," Anisha smiled, making a face at him–glad about the joke, glad that she could laugh at it and show everybody how childish she had been.

Her parents exchanged a look of relief over the cornflakes and porridge. Anisha was being her normal self again, she was smiling at Mihir's joke! Still, Mrs Banerjee made an effort and treated her son to a mild rebuke.

"Really, Mihir, is that any way to talk? He is a very nice boy. If they come again, you must be present and get to know him."

"Only if she agrees to marry him," Mihir said solemnly.

"Okay, that's enough," rapped out Mr Banerjee. The rest of the breakfast passed in innocuous small talk, with Mrs Banerjee imploring her husband not to spread his toast with so much butter, and pressing some more fruits on Mihir that she had cut specially for him. Then father and son left for office together and Anisha, her smiling, obsequious equilibrium quite restored, got ready to go to her art class.

Two days later the news came. It was wonderful, joyful news, yet Mrs Banerjee thought it prudent to break it only after she had discussed it with her husband. In the evening they summoned Anisha to their bedroom. Mr Banerjee was looking expansive in his arm chair and Mrs Banerjee was sitting straight-backed on the bed. They received their daughter, smiling like a pair of potentates about to hand out a prize. Then Mr Banerjee cleared his throat and began, "Anisha, we have some very good news. Mrs Lahiri called Ma today and said they really liked you. They are very interested in this match."

Anisha could not believe her ears. "But...but...what about my horoscope?" she stammered.

Mrs Banerjee opened her mouth to speak and then closed it as they had agreed that Mr Banerjee would do the talking. And so he did. He looked at his daughter affectionately, and gave a little chortle of delight, "Well, what do you think? We told them your birth time. They've had it analysed by their family astrologer. It turns out that the boy's horoscope and yours are quite well-matched. He is also a er..."

"Rakshas Gon," Mrs Banerjee prompted with an air of triumph.

"But that's not all. His horoscope is a perfect fit with yours in many other ways. You'll make a very happy pair. And I'll give you some more good news," Mr Banerjee said. "They don't mind if you work after marriage. You always wanted to work, didn't you? Now you can do your BEd and teach in a school."

Anisha was quite numb with shock. "But I don't like this man, Baba," she said to her father. "I don't want to marry him. He's...he's so uncouth, so dark...I don't think I shall be happy with him if I dislike him so much."

Her parents tried to reason with her. They tried to explain that this match was no less than heaven-sent. Didn't she know what a difficult horoscope she had, and how many families had shied away from her (even though she was so pretty and accomplished) because of it? She had a serious handicap, for god's sake! She couldn't afford to be so picky! The boy was qualified, had a decent job, came from a good family–what more did she want? Dark, fair, these were superficial things–how could she be so childish as to say that she didn't like him for such a silly reason? She didn't even know him. She may like him a lot once she got to know him.

"And if I still don't like him? Will you want me to marry him even then," Anisha asked quietly. Tears had sprung to her eyes but they remained unshed, locked in her flaming sockets as she regarded her parents. They were like a pair of good cop and bad cop, it suddenly occurred to her, and she wondered why she had never noticed it before.

"Yes we will," snapped Mrs Banerjee. "We have no wish to have you sit on our heads all our lives! And it isn't as if you'll ever be able to find someone on your own steam! We put you in a co-ed college, but did anything come of it? Did you manage to get yourself a boy? No, you did not! Now Surajit is a very good boy. And you shall marry him if by god's grace there are no other issues. They are very keen to have an alliance with our family. After all, Baba's position is not to be scoffed at. It's only because of your wretched horoscope that it's taken this long to find someone for you."

The wedding was fixed fairly quickly. There were a few questions about what kind of monetary settlement the Banerjees would make on their daughter. (Being cultured Bengalis, the Lahiris would never ask for a dowry, but they wanted to make sure that their future daughter-in-law was well provided for.) Once that was resolved to the satisfaction of both families, the wedding date too was decided.

Anisha and Surajit met a few more times, although it was understood that she, rather than he, was on trial. Even at this stage, he could refuse to have her if he so desired. Anisha could claim no such privilege. So she took a deep breath and steeled herself to try and like this man. After all, she had been prepared to like whoever her parents chose for her. But it was no good. She found him as repulsive as she had on that first occasion. It was not just his physical appearance and his less than perfect diction. She found him petty and pugnacious. On their third meeting, he told her that he was happy that she was 'convent-educated', but hoped that she did not have any Western airs and graces.

"What do you mean," Anisha asked meekly.

"We are a simple Bengali family and we don't like people who are always doing *phatar phatar* in English."

At their next meeting, he mentioned that he made it a point never to have an argument with anyone. "Especially not if he's my boss," he smiled craftily. "But if someone tries to get the better of me, I fix him sooner or later."

Anisha felt that she had never met a more unpleasant person in her life.

There were a few more scenes with her parents. She broke down and begged them not to force her into this marriage. Her father looked miserable and guilty. Her mother blazed at her for her unimaginable stupidity.

"Why can't I remain unmarried," she cried. "I want to stay unmarried! Please just let me be!"

"Oh yes, and have all our relatives say that we couldn't get you married off," sniffed her mother. "Enough is enough. You are getting married to Surajit. It'll be best for everyone if you get used to the idea."

She supposed she could have left home. Or found a job and left home. People did. Even her brother told her, "Look, if you dislike him so much, just put your foot down, okay? Say you won't do it. They can't force you bodily as if you're a bloody village girl!"

But Anisha said nothing more. She could not go against her parents' wishes. That impulse had been broken and pulverised in her long ago. So she sank into a numb silence and waited for the inevitable like an animal who knows it is about to be sacrificed.

Then slowly something changed. Amidst the sarees and the jewellery, and the wedding cards being given for printing, and talk of whether there should be golden fried prawns on the menu and perhaps a pre-wedding cocktail just for Mr Banerjee's colleagues and their more affluent relatives—a little fire was born in Anisha's mind. It sparked and flared and prompted an incredible thought. If the stars had given her such power to do evil, why couldn't she contrive to make something bad happen to the man who was to wed her? Maybe she could put a hex on him, think him into some sort of an injury–kill him even. That would surely put a stop to this wedding. If she focused her mind on the thought really, really hard, maybe the deed would be done. The only hitch was that he was supposed to be her perfect match, so her psychic efforts to destroy him might not work.

Well, then, Anisha brooded calmly, why not concentrate on his parents? She knew that if there was a death in the groom's family, the wedding would certainly be cancelled. Oh yes, she thought with relief, thanking heaven that she had found a way out of her awful predicament. She only had to throw her black-hearted malevolence at them and one of them would be dead, dead, dead!

The wedding was barely a month away. Anisha seemed to be sleepwalking through the complicated process of mounting a wedding that would do justice to her father's 'position'. When she was not being buffed and polished for the big day - going through hair spas and facials that were guaranteed to give her that pre-orgasmic bridal glow - she remained closeted in her room, her burning eyes fixed on her goal, her feverish mind trained on the job at hand. She who had attenuated her will almost to vanishing point, she who had never hated anybody or anything with passion, reached deep into herself and dredged up a virulent tide of anger and hate. Let something bad happen to Mr Lahiri or Mrs Lahiri, she prayed obsessively. Or better still, let that man perish! She wished them gone, vaporised, and turned to God or Devil to grant her the wish.

Four days before the wedding, Mr Banerjee was sitting on his cane chair and making some wedding expense related calculations when he suddenly clutched his chest and fell over on the floor. Mrs Banerjee heard the crash and came running. She let out a long and terrifying howl and everyone rushed to see what the matter was. Mr Banerjee was conscious, but sweating profusely. The pressure on his chest made him gasp for breath. An ambulance was called and he was quickly stretchered into it. Mrs Banerjee too got in. Her face was ashen, her lips drawn tight like a tribal death mask. Before getting into the ambulance, she turned her terrible eyes on Anisha and whispered, "So you have done it at last! You have eaten your own father!"

Anisha stared at her. Her mother looked dreadful, she thought—like a savage deity with a licence to kill. Yet for the first time, she felt curiously light-hearted and free. The acid rain of her mother's words dripped off her and she emerged from it whole and unstained. This proved that they had all been wrong, she exulted. She had no evil powers at all! Her horoscope was a hoax and her cursed influence a rotten lie! She had wished those others dead—certainly not her own father!

But oh, what if the missile of her curse got misdirected? Could it have slammed into her father instead of its intended victims? No, that was impossible! Things weren't supposed to work that way! But even if that were so, it couldn't be helped, and she almost shrugged her small shoulders. At least the wedding would be called off now. She smiled a hard, sweet smile at the thought, watching the ambulance move off with its siren wailing, its ball of light flashing, watching it cleave through the traffic like a pathfinder parting the sea, as her father lay living or dying and the stars above glittered and glowered.

That Cabbie

Manjira was late for work. She disliked being late for anything, most of all, for work. And today was an important day. Her event management company was about to score a huge triumph. She had a video conference lined up with the bigwigs at the Vienna Philharmonic Orchestra to put the final touches on the plan to bring the orchestra to Kolkata and Mumbai. The representatives of the two main sponsors would be there as well. She had been working on this project for months, and now it was almost a done deal. If she pulled it off, it would mean that she had arrived. After this, her Flash First event management company was sure to be up there among the best in the country.

So naturally, Manjira was in a state of high excitement. Which was probably why she could not find her latch key when she was about to leave for work. When several minutes of frantic search did not reveal the truant key, she stuck her head into her mother's bedroom where the 76-year-old Mrs Dutt, attired in her blue nightgown, was sitting in an armchair, eating her porridge and watching a breakfast show on TV. A maid hovered in attendance, making the bed while she was about it. Manjira told her mother that she could not find her key.

"But I have to leave now," she said. "I have a very important meeting today."

As she had expected, a faint note of shrillness crept into Mrs Dutt's voice at once. "But Manji, you have to find it," she said. "We can't possibly let the door key fall into the hands of a servant!"

Manjira was embarrassed because she was sure that the maid could follow the general drift of an English conversation. But Mrs Dutt swept on: "You must find it before you leave. Otherwise I shall be worried all day. And you know I am going to Khuku Pishi's for lunch. I couldn't possibly go knowing that a servant could have got hold of the door key and was probably getting a copy made!"

Manjira felt her anger rising, as it often did during the mostly futile arguments she had with her mother. She was always a bit shamed by her mother's calm assumption that the 'lower classes' were out to rob and cheat people like them. And it shamed and annoyed her even more because Mrs Dutt aired her views with such nonchalance in front of their domestic helps. She liked to think of herself as a left-leaning liberal and she felt that her mother's studied class consciousness was a direct attack on her own sensibilities. It was almost as if Mrs Dutt was intent on showing that she didn't give a toffee for her daughter's enlightened world view. As far as she was concerned, the world was divided into two vastly different, and warring, groups–the upper classes and the lower classes, us and them. And to Mrs Dutt, the 'us' were unfailingly superior to the thieving, villainous 'them'.

Really, her mother was quite impossible, thought Manjira, and tsked in irritation. She felt like slamming the door on her face and leaving for work–key or no key. But she knew that if she left without the key being found, Mrs Dutt would call her a dozen times during the day. If she did not take her calls, she would ring up on her office landline and leave urgent messages with her two assistants. She would sound imperious and injured, like a queen who had fallen on hard times. Coupled with her 1950s la-di-da Loreto House accent, it was quite an act. And few things infuriated Manjira more than her mother's 'aggrieved hauteur' performance for the benefit of her colleagues.

So she looked at her watch, and said, "All right, I'll look for the key for another 10 minutes. If I still don't find it, tough luck–I absolutely must leave."

"Well, there's no need to take that attitude, you know," Mrs Dutt said coldly. "No call for that sharpness of tone. Do leave right now if you wish to."

Happily, the key was found a few minutes later. Stuck to its cheap 'I Love NY' key chain – one of those trinkets that friends and relatives felt obliged to bring back for you from their forays in foreign lands – it had been lying in Manjira's soft black leather bag all the time. Yet she could have sworn that she had dug her hand into every compartment of the bag at least twice before to check if it was there.

Her mother pacified and the key safely stowed away in her bag once again, it was 9.50 when Manjira finally stepped out. She was running 20 minutes late, she noted. It didn't mean that she was late for her video conference. That was not until two in the afternoon and it was to be held in the office of a media house, which was one of the main sponsors. But running behind schedule stressed her out. On top of that, today the lift seemed to be taking an awfully long time to go down the nine floors. Her lips thinned in annoyance each time it jerked to a halt at a floor. On two occasions, no one entered at all. This irritated her even more. "I'm getting old," she scolded herself, "Old, irritable and impatient. In 20 years, I shall be just as impossible as Ma."

Manjira was 47. Once pretty, her face and figure had thickened considerably over the years. She had deep dark circles around her kohl-lined eyes, which made her round face look slightly like a raccoon's. Always partial to trousers, she had taken to wearing long, billowy shirts with them in an effort to hide her middle-age spread. When she dressed in a saree, which was not often, she looked every bit the heavy-bosomed, broad-hipped matron. But in her flowy printed crepe top, cropped trousers, dainty peep-toes, bobbed hair and a long string of beads looped around her neck, she looked smart and trendy. She was middle-aged, yes. Frumpy, no.

She had never got around to marrying. Though she had known many men, and had gone to bed with some of them, marriage had always been contemplated—never actually decided on. She didn't mind her singlehood. Not too much, that is. Sometimes she thought that it might have been nicer to have had her own family and her own home. Living with her mother was a strain. But then, for all you knew, tolerating a husband might have been even more strenuous.

Her work sustained her, and she had some good friends to hang out with. At parties, ad agency dos and club nights where she sat with her chums, she often joked, "There's nothing to beat life as a singleton. My only regret is that I don't have a handy toy boy—you know, a nice no-strings-attached carnal relationship!"

"Heh, heh," her friends laughed their slightly drunken party laugh. "There, how about that guy over there," someone cackled. And Manjira rolled her eyes and completed the routine. "Um, not bad. Good bod. But he probably has halitosis. There's always some awful, non-negotiable minus point in good looking men!"

She came out of her building gate and began to walk towards the main road. There were usually two or three cabs parked there at this time of the day. It was 'office-time', as the rush hour between 9 and 11 in the morning was called. So the cabs didn't have to wait too long for a fare. Manjira had a beat-up Honda Jazz and a part-time driver who came around three times a week. But the car was mainly for Mrs Dutt's use, and for the driver to scrape and batter at will. Manjira preferred to cab it to office and back.

As she had expected, there were a couple of Ambassador taxis crouching in the hot sun like lazy yellow slugs. She couldn't quite make out if her favourite cabbie was there today. For she had a favourite—a young man who drove a yellow taxi with the legend 'hypothecated to Allahabad Bank, Sodepur Branch' scrawled on its back.

On most days of the week, she found him waiting at that unofficial taxi stand. If he was there, she invariably hopped into his cab. She had used him so many times in the last few months that he almost felt like a personal chauffeur now. He drove reasonably well, took her straight to her office in Park Circus, knew which route she liked best, and treated her with respect and courtesy. She had tried the cabs you had to call through mobile apps. But she found the process a bother, and preferred her regular cabbie who didn't have to be directed to her destination in spite of Google Maps.

Manjira did not know the man's name. She thought it would be nice to know his name since she used him so often. But a certain reserve, a sense that asking the young man his name would make for a kind of familiarity between them, stopped her from asking it. She didn't even know his face very well. She knew that it was the face of a man in his mid to late 20s, darkish, with the shadow of a stubble on his cheeks. He had high cheek bones, a pleasant mouth, and a jutting, somewhat aggressive, jawline. Actually, she knew the back of his head much better than she knew his face. She often found herself staring at it and at the way his hair sprang glossy and abundant from his short, thick neck.

He wore shabby shirts with frayed collars or round-necked T-shirts. Sometimes her eyes wandered towards his wiry, hairless arms and the hint of muscle tightening under his half-sleeved shirt as he swung the steering wheel around. He had a habit of resting his left hand on his left thigh when they hit a clear road and he didn't need to change gears too often. She felt a bit uncomfortable when he did that. But she did not say anything. She just watched his hand as it lay prone on his tight young thigh. It was a medium sized hand with short, stubby fingers. He wore a tarnished silver ring with a dark brown gemstone on the ring finger of his left hand. Strange, how even a cabbie goes to astrologers and wears gems to turn his luck. What did he want? The usual things, she supposed–more money, a better life. Perhaps a fleet of taxis all his own!

Shantanu, her last boyfriend, had not believed in the magical power of gemstones. The cabbie often made her think of him. He had the same kind of short and thick fingers. A bit working class, she used to think when she was having an affair with him. But he was good with those fingers, oh yes, he was! Shantanu, married with two children, committing adultery with Manjira in a Loudon Street hotel room, could make her writhe and groan with his short, stubby fingers.

Well, that skunk certainly ditched her nice and proper, didn't he? He told her that his wife had threatened suicide if he did not break up with her. Suicide, for the love of god! It wasn't as if they were in love with each other! Or wanted to marry! Yet she had been livid when he came around with a sheepish look and said they'd have to stop meeting because his wife had found out about them. What a cad Shantanu was! What a cowardly, duplicitous hypocrite!

At times Manjira wondered idly if the cabbie would fit that toy boy persona she liked to joke about at parties. If she did not have a packed day ahead, she sometimes let her mind nibble at the thought. It was never a full blown fantasy with all the details filled out in lurid technicolour. It was just a fleeting vision of a what-if kind of possibility. The cabbie wasn't unpleasant to look at. And he didn't smell, thank god. Some of these lower classes smell, well, so unwashed. Okay, so that sounded exactly like something her mother would say, Manjira thought and grinned inwardly. But really, BO was not something she could put up with. The cabbie seemed odourless, which made the fantasy seem almost workable.

Of course, the very thought was preposterous–a taxi driver, for crissakes! It was never going to happen! It was an impossible scenario, like a C-grade Bollywood masala movie! Even there, the taxi driver whom the heroine romances invariably turns out to be the long-lost son of a tycoon! And pairing an older woman with a poor cabbie? That would never do, would it? She laughed at herself for her sinful cougar woman instincts. Still, her mind darted around the idea. Sitting on the back seat, with the traffic up ahead and behind the vehicle seeming to push the two of them closer, she often wondered vaguely if the cabbie might be a good fuck.

And what would her mother say if she knew that Manjira could even contemplate such an idea? The superior Mrs Dutt, always super conscious of her aristocratic lineage and the things she and her family could and could not do, would probably pass out in shock. And that amused Manjira no end.

She walked quickly towards the taxi stand, glancing at her watch again as she did so. She was late, late, whirred a tiny alarm inside her. And the traffic would only get worse now. She saw that her favourite cabbie was there after all. He was slouching against his taxi, chatting with another man. When he saw Manjira approaching, he straightened up expectantly. She was a few feet from him when she heard the other man chuckling, "Go on, there comes your *khodder*–your client."

Manjira stopped in her tracks for a fraction of a second. She felt her ears burn. What was it that the man just said? It was some unspeakable insult, she was sure of that. His smirk, his mocking tone, made it clear that it was. And he had winked too–a slow, evil wink that was like a slap on her face. Her first impulse was to turn back and find another taxi. Or maybe she could take out her own car, she thought. But she was a shaky driver and she was late! She couldn't afford to be late today, she thought, and got inside the cab briskly.

"Office, Madam," asked the cabbie.

"Yes."

The cab moved off. The sun was hot now and it lay hazy and yellow on the multi-storied houses on both sides of Ballygunge Circular Road. She rolled up the glass to block out the dusty, polluted air that stank of heat and hell black fumes. But the pollution charged right back in through the open windows in the front and she sat enveloped in its dense, acrid fug, trying to calm her fury at what the man had just said.

This was turning out to be one of those days when things went wrong somehow. And the traffic! It was simply crawling! They had been stuck at a four-way crossing for a very long time. Would the dimwit cop ever manage to flick the green light on, she wondered wrathfully. She was convinced that it was just mismanagement that created these godawful traffic snarl-ups. Really, any halfway decent traffic expert could straighten things out! But the whole system was built on inefficiency, she fumed—government, police, everything, everything in this wretched city was so bloody screwed up!

They inched along Ballygunge Circular Road. How the area had changed, Manjira thought with disgust not for the first time. She remembered so many houses on this road. Their own ancestral home, now sold and rebuilt as an apartment block, was down that lane. They were big, airy bungalows with porticos and outhouses and driveways laid with smooth pink gravel. There were neat lawns where children would put up the nets and play badminton in the evenings. But the fortunes of the families they housed slowly went downhill. They crumbled with genteel regret and were sold off one by one—the green and the gracious living gobbled up by the ever-spreading torrent of tall rich men's tenements.

Manjira did not usually feel elegiac about the past. That was her mother's forte, she thought with a grimace. She didn't want to be regressive, looking back instead of looking ahead. It was a sure sign of age when you felt that way. And today of all days she ought not to be sighing and moaning about the past. She had a great present, goddammit! She was on the verge of a big achievement. I'll celebrate tonight if the VC goes well and we put the deal in the bag, she thought. She would call some friends over to the club and do some serious carousing. Fingers crossed.

Her cell phone rang. It was Ishita, her assistant. She was calling to find out why Manjira was late. "Yes, Ishita. Stuck in a terrible jam," Manjira said, using the brisk tone she reserved for her subordinates. "But I think I should be there in the next 20 minutes. Just keep the final slides and printouts on my table, please. Yup. Thanks."

She made an effort to compose herself and focus on the important work ahead. Well, she had her presentation ready. Both sides had agreed upon the Vienna Philharmonic's India itinerary. Now it was just a question of tying up the loose ends, making sure that the sponsors in Mumbai and Kolkata stuck to their part of the bargain, and creating an atmosphere of bonhomie all around. But she needed to get to her office, sit at her desk and collect her thoughts! And it was nearing 11 now! She was late, late, Manjira panicked, and she would be even more so because the traffic was barely moving today.

"Are you getting late for an appointment, Madam," asked the cabbie, looking at her through the rear view mirror.

"Yes, I am. I have something very important today. Can't afford to be late for it," she said, looking back into his eyes in the mirror.

"After this signal we should get a clear stretch," he told her in an even, mild voice.

Manjira was touched that he had noticed her agitation and was trying to reassure her. He's a good chap, she thought, and that's why I don't take those anonymous AC cabs with their clueless drivers. And then her mind went scurrying back to the man at the taxi stand. What was it that he had called her? A client—a *khodder*. Well, in a sense, she *was* the cabbie's client. She was his fare. Then why did she feel as if she had been violated, as if she had been sullied and soiled? What an awful word—*khodder!* And the way he uttered it! As though she were buying the cabbie's services for something else! Oh lord, did the cabbie and his pals think that she was sexually interested in him? All because she had shown a preference for him? Or had they looked inside her head and seen the secret garden of her fantasies?

Sweat ran down her face and her clothes stuck to her body. Her carefully blow-dried hair hung limp. Oh, the day was ruined,

Manjira thought desperately. It was ruined the moment that leering, sneering man at the taxi stand made his disgusting insinuation! Her eyes went to the cabbie's short, fleshy neck, the neck she had looked at so many times. She saw the runnels of perspiration there and a faint ridge of dirt just above his collar. How dirty his collar was too! And they thought that she, Manjira Dutt, who was once the belle of Ballygunge and could have had her pick of men, would seriously lust after a dirty rotten taxi driver?

She sat stewing in her fantastic outrage, aware all the while that the clock was ticking away like a time bomb. Suddenly, the cabbie swerved to change lanes, as impatient, lawless drivers often will, and another vehicle rammed into it.

The cabbie switched off the ignition at once and jumped out of the car.

"You @#**," he shouted at the driver of the other car. This too was a taxi and its driver was out of the car instantly, almost as if he couldn't wait to have a brawl under the boiling sun.

Manjira, unhurt but somewhat shaken, saw that the other taxi also had a lone passenger who was sitting woodenly inside. Both the drivers were screaming now, their sweaty faces close to each other. They were locked in a pantomime of fury, their raw expletives soundless in the ear-splitting blare of horns. The traffic piled up behind them and people stuck their heads out of car windows and shouted at them to break it up and move along.

Manjira's cell phone began to ring again. She let it ring in her bag and got out of the car. This was intolerable, she thought frantically. She had to stop this altercation right now and get going. Out of the corner of her eye, she saw a white-helmeted cop with a large, pendulous belly and a belt stuck just above his crotch, sauntering towards them.

"Come on, enough, leave it and let's go," she said to her cabbie.

The other driver, a thin, ferrety man wearing a purple T-shirt that was dark with perspiration, turned to face her.

"*Aei*, he can leave it, but *shono*, listen, I won't," he screamed, using the familiar form of address instead of the polite, formal one. "What about the damage to my car, *hain? Tumi debey*, will you pay for the damage he's done, *hain? Eeeh*, she's come to do *dalali* for him!"

She saw the specks of foam on his vicious mouth and the snarl of insult on his face. She was suddenly seized with a red hot rage at the monstrous unjustness of it all. The next moment she slapped him hard, her arm swinging out in violent reflex from her need to hit out–at this horrid scum of a man, at her ruined day, at the sniggers and the winks, at the past which was gone and the future that would never be.

Someone was twisting her arm and fingers like hot iron clips were clasped around her throat. Her head jerked back and she was choking, fighting to breathe. Now the cop was upon them in a blur of white. People rushed in and the man was pulled away from her, and there was a great hubbub all around.

"I'll get even with that *maagi*–that bitch," the man shouted, and Manjira heard the cop roaring at him. She was coughing and feeling her throat, as if to make sure that it was still there. Another policeman had joined them by now, and he was ticking her off for starting the fight, while her cabbie stood there, open-mouthed with shock.

Then a kind looking man with a ragged moustache said, "Didi, are you okay? Times are not good, you shouldn't get into fights with such ruffians."

Manjira smiled at him. The furious ringing in her ears was slowing now. She wanted to tell him that she was fine. She had never felt finer in her life.

April is a Cruel Month

It was turning out to be an unusually mild April. The days were warm and bright. But evening brought lowering clouds that rumbled darkly and blew a gust of storm. It was never a full-throated tempest or a Kaal Baishakhi that boiled over after days of stifling heat. And nor did the rain come blistering down, smiting the dusty earth and sending quick-flowing currents of muddy water along the gutters. Still, the almost daily event of a muted storm followed by a light shower cooled the evenings and turned the nights soft and balmy.

"What a lovely beginning to summer!" Rafi exclaimed, throwing his arms around his wife. And Sona, or Ayesha, as she was supposed to be called now, smiled in acquiescence and offered her face to him for a kiss.

Privately, Sona did not care too much for this particular summer. In the small, stuffy bedroom of Rafi's single-storied house in Howrah, April felt hotter than she had ever known it to be. The heat closed in upon her even as the ancient fan clack-clacked resolutely and churned the steamy air. It didn't help that the room was dark and you had to keep the tube light switched on throughout the day. The fluorescent light trickled off the pistachio green, distemper-washed walls and gave the room a sickly, bilious pallor. The windows too offered no break from the gloom. Barred by iron rods rusty with age, one of them faced a neighbour's crumbling, graffiti-scrawled boundary wall, and the other looked out into an unrelieved vista of concrete, punctuated with tall black factory chimneys that smoked vilely all day long.

It had not been half as bad in autumn and winter. But it was different now. Sona looked around the cramped room that lay listless and clammy in its greenish-white hospital light and struggled against the claustrophobia and heat that threatened to overwhelm her.

Rafi had wanted to install an air-conditioner in the bedroom immediately after they got married. But Sona would have none of it. She was filled with love for her husband and intoxicated with her courage and daring at having married him. It elevated her in her own eyes and in the fire of her noble emotion she had declared that she would live exactly the way the rest of his family did, that is, without such luxuries as ACs.

Rafi's mother Ruksana and brother Siraj had been moved almost to tears by her words.

"A girl from such a rich family," they said again and again to anybody who cared to listen. "And look how humble and down-to-earth she is!"

In truth, they treated her like a princess in exile, or like an honoured guest who had stopped by for a while. When she went into their dingy kitchen and flopped down on the floor to roll the *chapatis*, Ruksana – a morose, shrivelled woman who regarded incessant physical labour to be her given lot – cried out in consternation and led Sona out of the kitchen. There was the same indignant response when Sona offered to scrub the pots and pans sitting down in the small, moss-laden backyard. The senior Mrs Alam, her eyes welling up at the goodness and generosity of her daughter-in-law, scotched the idea at once. To the Alams, the whole thing was still quite incredible. They were all slightly awed by Sona, awed by the fact that this 23-year-old girl, whose father was a millionaire many times over, had come to live with them in their bleak, soot-blackened house slap bang in the middle of the industrial sprawl of Howrah.

Sona's father was a tall, big-built man with small, veiled eyes and a laugh that started slow and disappeared before it had quite got there. He had made his pile in the construction business. He had interests in coal and steel as well, and lately, he had ventured into the booming arena of private hospitals sprouting at lightning speed on the outskirts of Kolkata. He was not famous, but he had made famous and important friends. Those who knew Dinu Chaudhury said that he had several top politicians, bureaucrats and policemen in his pocket. He had mastered the art of prospering in an otherwise stagnant Bengal, and he pursued his legal and illegal businesses with such oily cunning and cold ruthlessness that over the last 20 years he had grown to be a very wealthy man.

At home, he was an affectionate husband and father who treated his placid wife with friendly indulgence and his son with occasional gruffness–as he felt that the 13-year-old boy needed some toughening up. His favourite, though, was his daughter. He adored Sona and there was little that he would not do to make her happy. That was probably why Sona had thought that he would come round and accept her marriage to Rafi. However, she had miscalculated the quality of his father's love for her. After a few moments of stunned silence at the news of her unbelievable act, Dinu Chaudhury had set all his resources into motion to try and reverse it.

Sona had met Rafi at the French language institute. At first her father had been reluctant to let her join it. He regarded a co-educational set-up with deep suspicion and Sona had always attended all-girls institutions. But now she had completed her bachelor's degree (a feat that made him swell with pride as she was the first graduate in the family) and was at a loose end. She had no wish to study any further. And while they were looking for a match for her, she chafed at the hours of idleness in the house. Learning French seemed like a nice and fashionable hobby. Her father suggested that she learn embroidery or take guitar lessons at home. But Sona was adamant. So many of her friends were learning French, she said. Why should she be the only one to be stuck in the house, she sulked. Honestly, Baba was just too old-fashioned, she fumed. So finally, her father gave in. "*Thik achhe-re baba*, once she's got something into her head, my Sona-rani has to have it, isn't it?" he said, shaking his massive bald head at her like a rhino in a playful mood.

It turned out that Dinu Chaudhury's fears about sending out his daughter amidst a 'pack of boys' had not been unjustified. For almost immediately after joining the French institute, Sona, the shy girl who was sober of dress and meek of deportment, fell violently in love. Rafi happened to her the way a fire happens to a tinder-dry forest—one spark and off it went, a vast and voracious thing, crackling through her and consuming her nights and days.

Rafi was a couple of years older than Sona—a dark, slender young man with a head full of wavy hair that he had a habit of running his hand through whenever he was thoughtful. He wore rectangular, black-rimmed glasses, was always dressed in a half-sleeved shirt, jeans and dirty grey sneakers, and carried a backpack slung over his shoulders. He looked earnest and academic—like a studious college boy. He had a masters degree in Political Science, and had decided to learn a foreign language while he was looking for a job and studying for competitive exams, which, *inshallah*, would be his passport to a career as a bureaucrat.

Rafi quickly became the star of the class. While others struggled to pronounce their 'je's and 'retrouve's, Rafi's felicitous tongue embraced the language as if he had been born to it. And Sona, who had always dreamed of an exciting love affair, anointed him in the role of a lover almost at once.

It was just a wild fantasy in her mind at first, for she had not hoped to catch his attention. She knew that men rarely looked at her twice. It was not just that she was plain–with a round, unremarkable face, a blunt nose, and ill-defined lips that flared slightly to reveal her somewhat prominent teeth. She failed to be a hit with the opposite sex chiefly because she was stiff and tongue-tied, and unschooled in the fine art of appearing coquettish or desirable. She didn't even know how to show off her long, straight hair – her one claim to beauty – and kept it tied in a single, severe plait.

And yet, Rafi noticed her. He spoke to her kindly and helped her with her lessons. When he leaned towards her to correct her conjugation or explain a point of French grammar, and she breathed his strange, unknown smell, her heart raced and bumped loudly in her chest. Maybe Rafi had sensed the way she thrilled to him. Maybe he had looked up and seen the soft delirium in her eyes. They quickly became close, closer than Sona had dared to imagine in her wildest dreams of love.

They often slipped out before getting into class and went walking on the Maidan. Or they went to the Victoria Memorial grounds. They sat on a bench amid a hundred other furtive couples, kissing and fondling and clinging to each other and the bit of green that hid them from a city that gave them no space. Rafi took her to see English films. He caressed her sparkling hair and recited the poems of Pablo Neruda to her. And Sona felt that she had breached the dull membrane of her existence and had stepped into a brave new world full of starburst and light.

Her parents suspected nothing. She had taken care to bribe the chauffeur who drove her to the language institute. She gave him a substantial part of her weekly allowance so he would not report her romance to her father. (This she did with admirable adroitness and nonchalance as she was, after all, the daughter of Dinu Chaudhury.) She was happy and serene at home. When asked to appear before a prospective groom and his family, she did so without protest. She had made up her mind to cross the bridge called arranged marriage if she came to it. But fortunately, that bridge had not materialised yet. None of these possible matches worked out—either because she did not like the boy or they did not like her, or because Dinu Chaudhury thought that his little girl deserved someone better.

It was all going her way, Sona congratulated herself smugly yet again, as she served her father some of the sweets that had been brought for the people who had come to 'see' her. The family had left after an unproductive exchange of strained small talk. Dinu Chaudhury, dressed in a sleeveless white vest and a green and white checked *lungi*, had lowered his bulk into his cavernous easy chair, and was fulminating against another encounter with another witless boy and his witless family. He railed at their impossible arrogance and then turned his ire on the state of Bengal. "The good boys have simply left this rotten place," he growled.

Sona giggled and massaged her father's neck and shoulders until he calmed down. Then he patted her hand and bellowed that he would get the best for his pet yet—"just you wait!" And Sona smiled with her father's veiled eyes, swimming in her well of forbidden feeling, steeped in her ecstatic present and uncaring of what her future might bring.

Today, nearly six months after her shock marriage to Rafi, Sona wondered if she had let her feeling run away with her. Had she been too hasty–too impulsive and thoughtless? She had discovered a vein of daring in herself that she never knew existed. It prompted her to do strange, astonishing things. Proposing marriage to Rafi the moment he got a job as a management trainee in a small business house was probably the most astonishing of them all.

Rafi had stared at her as if she had taken leave of her senses.

"Are you serious? You know that's impossible! Your parents would never accept it. My mother might, but not your folks!"

They had often discussed marriage, of course. But Rafi had always spoken of it as a sort of wistful neverland that would shimmer in the distance forever. It simply wasn't meant to be! They were separated by a million divides: he a Muslim, she a Hindu; she enjoyed all the luxuries that her crorepati dad could buy her, whereas his family lived on the widow's pension of his mother after his father died wearing himself out in a minor government job; she, poised to become the wife of a wealthy man, and he, busing it to his Rs 18,000 a month trainee executive's job and hoping to crack the IAS exam this second time.

So even as Rafi spoke to Sona of love, he knew that theirs was merely a romantic interlude before life took over and ground it under its feet. They were 'girlfriend and boyfriend' - forever and eternally - and their story would be no different to a thousand other unfinished love stories that fell by the grounds of Victoria

Memorial every day. She would marry someone else and perhaps he would shed a tear for what might have been. In fact, to Rafi, the inevitability of their parting gave their relationship a certain tragic glamour, a sad glow of loss, that appealed to his sensitive and sentimental nature.

But there was Sona now, suggesting that they throw familial wrath and social censure to the winds and actually get married.

"I can't bear the thought of marrying anyone else. I can't live without you," she said, choking into her fluent tears. "Now that you have a job, what's to prevent us? Let's just run away and get married!"

Rafi was powerless before the storm of her emotion. He continued arguing feebly for some weeks, feeling cowardly and unlover-like as he did so. He pointed out how utterly impossible it was. Sona was used to a certain lifestyle. He would not be able to provide even a fraction of the comforts she was used to, he said again and again. Besides, his job was just a temporary arrangement—he didn't plan to work there for very long. He was really aiming for higher things. Couldn't Sona wait then, wait until he got through the IAS?

No, no, she couldn't, she said. Her parents wouldn't wait and would force her to marry someone else. But she could only be happy with him! She would do everything for love, suffer anything at all—she would, she would, she said, raising her face to him and looking at him with such tremulous passion that her words did not seem the slightest bit artful or trite.

Finally, Rafi gave in. Not without trepidation perhaps, but convinced at last that whatever happened, marriage to the girl he had walked the Maidan with was a heroic and righteous act.

And oh, it was all so exciting, thought Sona, sitting at the chipped dresser in Rafi's bedroom. For a moment her face lit up at the memory and glowed anew in the spotted mirror. She had left her house with a small suitcase and told the watchman to call a taxi. He had looked at her askance, but had obeyed without a word. There was no one in the house to question where she was going. Her father was away at a construction site in Rajarhat, her mother was visiting a relative, and her brother was at school.

So off she went boldly into Rafi's waiting arms. And then, it was she and Rafi at the masjid before the quazi. She had got two of her oldest friends to stand witness to their *nikaah*. She gave up her religion without a second thought. Then the *nikaah* happened quickly, and there she was - suddenly, joyfully, irrevocably - Mrs Ayesha Alam!

They had arrived at Rafi's home in a taxi. His entire extended family turned up to welcome her. Sona was dressed in an everyday salwar kameez, unadorned but for the garland of red roses that Rafi had given her. Yet she felt like a heroine in a movie—the girl who had left everything behind for the sake of love! Her only regret was that she did not get to have a grand wedding. But that was nothing, she had thought. That day and that night, and for several days thereafter, nothing, but nothing could dilute her joy. Her mother had erupted into hysterics when she called her in the evening to give her the news. Her father was speechless at first, and then conducted a cold and detailed interrogation about Rafi as if he were a dangerous disease that she had contracted. But Sona cared nothing for them or their rage. Her joy made her fearless and proud.

When Dinu Chaudhury's Tata Safari screeched to a halt before their doorstep the next day, and he jumped out with a couple of young thugs and a police constable demanding to see the scoundrel who had married his girl for her money, Sona pushed the quavering Ruksana inside and faced her father.

"I love my husband," she told him in a high, ringing voice, as the neighbours poured out of their narrow doors and windows to listen in.

"Don't try to intimidate us, Baba. I am happy here."

The veil over Dinu Chaudhury's eyes was off that day. His face was terrible, his eyes bulging and bloodshot. He clenched his teeth and spat out:

"You are a fool! But I'll see to that man. No one gets away with making a fool of my daughter!"

He got into his SUV and thundered away without a second glance at her. The constable stayed behind, and under his benign gaze, the two thugs delivered several kicks to the front door of Rafi's house. Then they hollered some abuse and went away. But when Rafi hurried back from office after getting frantic calls from his mother, they reappeared at once. They rounded on him, roughed him up, and broke his spectacles. The neighbours came to his rescue and a bruised and bleeding Rafi was helped into the house.

Even on that awful day Sona had felt strong and sure, as if she were at the centre of a violent drama whose outcome she could control. As Ruksana keened softly, and Rafi sat trembling, she felt that she was the rock in this traumatised household. Holding an ice pack to her husband's cut lip and bleeding nose, she said calmly, "Enough is enough. We have to go to the police."

Sona had been so amazingly brave, thought Rafi, as he walked down Park Street on his way to office on this sun-drenched April day. Through all the troubles of the last few months, he had never ceased to marvel at her strength and her spirit. Sona was really that–*sona*, solid gold!

A smile came to his lips when he thought of her. He had not wished to go to the police to complain against his father-in-law. After all, it was to be expected that a man like Dinu Chaudhury would be furious that his daughter had married not just a Muslim, but one who was without wealth and privilege. Rafi had hoped that he would forgive and forget with time.

Sona, though, had insisted on logging a police complaint. The goondas were in her father's pay, she told him. He used them often and she had seen them at their house a few times. "We have to go to the police. You don't know my father," she said. "If he has gone this far, he can do more."

So Rafi let Sona take him by the hand, and the two of them walked down the narrow, fetid lanes, where the smell of urine, and worse, rose perennially from open drains. They made their way to the local *thana*. Rafi was feeling naked and disoriented without his glasses and he held on to her hand as if she were his saviour.

At the police station, the officer-in-charge listened to their tale without a word. He kept chewing his *paan*, sending flecks of red spittle flying from his large, greedy mouth. Then he gave Rafi a long stare and said that a complaint had already been registered against him.

"What for," Rafi asked incredulously.

"For criminal conspiracy. For running away with a girl against her wish. In fact, you could be arrested if you're not careful."

It was preposterous, Rafi said, beginning to shake with rage. But Sona - who knew she was so pragmatic and wise! - was unruffled. She came out of the police station and told him that they would need to get hold of a lawyer right away.

"But it's such an outrageously baseless case! You are an adult! You can marry whoever you want! How can they possibly charge me with criminal conspiracy?"

Sona giggled.

"You don't know anything, do you? False cases are a dime a dozen. Do you know how many people lose their land and property through false cases? And then my father buys them cheap, bribes a whole lot of people, builds a multi-storey building there and makes pots of money."

Rafi walked slowly, cutting a careful furrow through the crowd of office-goers and jaywalking pedestrians. Something hard knocked against his leg. He looked up sharply, but it was only a man with a bulging briefcase–a man in a hurry, preoccupied, distracted, and not looking where he was going. Rafi relaxed and walked on.

The shops on both sides of Park Street were rolling back their shutters and opening up for business. That's a nice saree, he thought idly as he passed a shop window where a barefoot man was carefully draping a gorgeous midnight blue material onto a mannequin with mountainous breasts. Rafi wanted to buy Sona something for her birthday next week. Maybe he would come back and find out the price of that saree. He wished to give her something fine and expensive. She had given him so much, she had heaped her astounding love and devotion–not just on him, but on his family too!

He had been apprehensive about whether she would fit in and be happy in his humble home. His mother too had prophesied grimly that no good would come of Rafi marrying a rich girl who was bound to be horribly spoilt. Yet Sona had proved all of them wrong. No new bride could be more respectful and attentive to her husband's family, Rafi thought gratefully. She was always trying to help with the housework. She had even learnt to read the namaz!

His family was not overly religious. He and his brother rarely prayed formally and his mother prayed only a couple of times a day. They had never dreamed that Sona would want to join her mother-in-law in the ritual of Islamic prayers. But she did. She quickly learnt to recite the Surah Fatiha from the Koran and a couple of other surahs too. When Ruksana knelt down to offer her prayers, Sona did the same, covering her head, facing west, and praising Allah, and Mohammad, His Prophet.

Rafi knew this was something that pleased Ruksana enormously. It pleased him too, he supposed, even though he considered himself areligious. When he fondled her firm plump body at night, he chuckled at his good luck. He had once nursed a secret hope that his father-in-law would 'do' something for him. With all his contacts, Dinu Chaudhury could have got him a plum job somewhere. He knew now that that would not happen. In any case, Rafi thought, now that he knew Dinu Chaudhury's true colours, he didn't even want to have anything to do with him. Well, it didn't matter. So he had a semi-criminal for a father-in-law, but he sure had a one in a million wife! God willing, and with Sona by his side, he would make it on his own!

But Sona had been pensive and petulant of late, thought Rafi, as he reached his office and joined the queue for the lift that would take him to his place of work on the eighth floor of the building. He wondered what was bothering her. Things were better now, after all.

For months there had been those awful terror calls. Menacing voices threatened to beat him to a pulp for "looting the virtue of a good girl". On several occasions thin, feral youths with hair dyed a vicious red-brown and T-shirts stretched tight across their bony young chests, had collided with him on the road, throwing him off balance. They looked at him as if he were dead meat, muttered some filthy abuse, and melted into the crowd. The police had done nothing about it.

The only place where Rafi felt safe was his own locality as the goondas had taken to avoiding it. The local councillor had picked up the Sona-Rafi story and had assured them of his support. If there were any more unpleasant incidents in their area, the whole thing could blow up into a Hindu-Muslim issue. Maybe that is why Dinu Chaudhury had at last tired of his terror tactics, Rafi thought. The goons had stopped cropping up here and there, and he had stopped looking over his shoulders all the time. There was peace at last.

And yet, Sona seemed depressed. Oh, well, girls will have their moods, I guess, thought Rafi, and stepped into the elevator that quickly filled up and moved heavenward with its load of blank-faced humans.

Sona raised herself with an effort. She could hear her mother-in-law calling her. She grimaced, gathered up her dupatta and put it over her head. These days Ruksana had taken to asking Sona to give her a hand with this or that. She seemed to have at last got over treating her daughter-in-law like a fragile celebrity. It was what Sona had always wanted, of course, but strangely, it did not please her now. She began to feel irritated when asked to step into the oily, ill-lit kitchen to knead the *atta* dough or peel the potatoes. Her regular household duties were so far limited to hanging the clothes out to dry in the backyard. But she didn't care for this job either. She had begun to dread that slowly, her quota of housework would expand and engulf her. God, would she end up like Ruksana, toiling night and day in this gloomy house?

What this house needed was a professional overhaul, a thorough paint and repair job. She had spoken of it to Rafi, but he had laughed and said, where was the money?

"Just pray that I am able to get through IAS or, at least, the banking exam. Then I can take you out of here," he had said, drawing patterns into her hair that lay splayed over the pillow like the hood of a snake.

Oh, it was all too annoying, Sona thought. She had never dreamed that she would have to worry about money. It was all right in the early days of her marriage when everything was so gloriously exciting. The elopement, the outrage of her parents, her father's strong-arm methods to break up the marriage, the boldness with which she had stood up to him, and the way everyone admired her for it...She had loved the danger and the drama of it all and the way her body sang to Rafi when they were together in their tiny green bedroom. For months and months, everything had been so perfect! And then slowly, the euphoria began to drain away. It bewildered her to be caught in this disconcerting lull after the storm. Suddenly, her finest hour seemed over and done with, and it was all whittling away and settling down now into the cold reality of hanging clothes out to dry and not enough money to go around.

She had squirmed in embarrassment when some of her friends dropped in to see her. She took them to her bedroom and sat them down on her bed, as there was no sitting room in the house. And all the while they chatted, giving her news of who else was getting married and who had broken up with whom, and this new shop where you got really good 'suits', Sona was agitated and uncomfortable. She wished she could hide the chipped dresser, the shabby furniture, the red oxide floor that must have shone once upon a time, but was now veined with a thousand ugly cracks. It was not thus that she wanted her friends to see her – not in this room, not in this place – not in the midst of these green tube-lit walls that were peeling all over. She was puzzled why the thought never came to her before, and why, now that it had, it didn't seem the least bit petty or ignoble.

The worst of it was that she could see no end to this dreariness. She doubted if Rafi would ever get through the IAS, or even the banking exam, which was supposed to be his Plan B. He had been too worked up to study properly these last few months. Anyway, he hardly had any time for studies after he came home from work. If only her father had been a bit reasonable! She had thought – though she never told Rafi this – that Dinu Chaudhury would eventually forgive her marriage and set up his son-in-law in some business. She had been pretty sure that when the dust settled and the din of her sin died down, she and Rafi would go and live in their big house in New Alipore. But who knew her father could be so pig-headed!

He had continued to call her, of course. During the day, when Rafi was out, he called up sometimes to ask how she was and if she needed anything. He also told her again and again that she could come back home any time she wished.

"Everybody makes mistakes," he said repeatedly, his voice at once hard and gentle, like a battering ram that had learnt to sheathe its blows. "You come back and we will forget it ever happened."

Each time Sona insisted that she was very happy with her husband and content to be where she was. But she was tired now. She was tired and bored with the role-playing that had so exhilarated her once. And scared too of the terrible finality that seemed to be slowly closing in upon her.

She made up her mind suddenly to go and visit her parents. They asked her to whenever they called. But she had not gone all these months because Rafi was never included in the invitation. Oh, but so what, she thought impatiently now, almost angry with herself for not having gone sooner. She would go alone. It would be a relief to be back home for a while. Back where she belonged.

At three o'clock that afternoon, Sona went out. She dropped her eyes, smiled at Ruksana, and said, "Ammi, I'm going to my friend Mitali's house. I'll call Rafi and tell him if I get a bit late."

Her homecoming after six months created a stir. Her mother hugged her and started crying. The servants looked on curiously, as if they were trying to discern if the change in her religion had wrought any visible physical change in her.

"How could you do this to us," her mother cried, although her sorrow sounded a bit shallow after all these months.

Sona went up the stairs and made for their wide, sunny verandah. She had forgotten how the Krishnachura tree outside their house burst into fiery bloom in April, and how the pavement below became a blazing carpet of red-orange flowers. She sat in her usual chair and gazed at the tree top and its blood-bright shroud. How beautiful, she thought happily. How utterly, utterly beautiful!

Her mother gave orders for some snacks to be prepared for her. Then she sat beside her and asked, "Is your husband a good man? Does he love you truly?"

"I suppose he does," Sona replied, looking away.

"Do you have a photograph of him?"

"No, Ma, I don't."

Her mother looked disappointed.

Her brother came back from school and regarded her critically.

"So you're a Mozzie now," he remarked with hostility.

Sona made a face at him and asked him how many subjects he had flunked in his last exams.

She tucked into the *chirer pulao* and *aloor chop* that had been hastily made for her and began to feel as if she had never been away.

A little later, Dinu Chaudhury's Tata Safari stopped in front of their gate with screaming brakes. Sona looked at her mother.

"I called him," her mother said.

Dinu Chaudhury came up the stairs with his heavy tread and sat down before Sona. He was panting a little and did not say anything for a while.

Then he said softly, "We missed you."

Sona began to cry. She pushed away her plate, hid her face in her hands and her tears flowed like a river undammed.

Dinu Chaudhury waved his wife away. He drew his chair close to Sona and asked her gently, "Do you want to stay here for a few days?"

Sona nodded through her veil of tears.

"Good," he said. "You don't have to go back. I'll take care of everything."

Sona cried even more, thinking that this was the moment to tell him that she would go back–she would, she would! She was married to Rafi, wasn't she? But her grief confused and overwhelmed her and she said nothing.

Dinu Chaudhury got up after a while and went downstairs. When the sun had nearly set and the fire had gone out of the Krishnachura tree, Sona got up too. She went towards her old bedroom. On the way, she stopped by the banisters and looked down. In the hall below her father was talking to someone on his mobile phone. His rough voice was pitched low and his words were almost indistinct. Sona strained her ears to hear what he was saying.

"I don't want any complications, you understand?" Dinu Chaudhury said. "There should be nothing to link the job back to us. Take him some place far away and do it."

Do it...do it... The words echoed up to Sona and her heart give a terrified leap. She crept away to her room. She did not wish to hear anymore.

The Trip

"Come on, come on, hurry up, get up quickly, the train stops here for only 15 minutes."

Vijay was already on the train. He had hefted the bigger of the two Samsonite suitcases and was now gesturing to Lekha to hand him the smaller one. People were pushing and shoving to squeeze their way through the narrow doorway of the train–all trying to get in first as if their life depended on it. Lekha would have preferred to have let the others pass and then boarded the train. They had confirmed tickets after all. But there was Vijay blocking part of the corridor and adding to the scrum. Besides, it was embarrassing the way he kept shouting, "Come on, Come on". So there was nothing for it but to give him the suitcase and yank herself up the steps of Samta Express that was to take them from Gwalior to Delhi in about 5 hours.

She followed him down the narrow corridor of the AC two-tier coach. "It's seat numbers 7 and 8, 7 and 8," Vijay repeated loudly. He wheeled one suitcase with his left hand and held the railway e-ticket in his right. The duffel bag hung from his right shoulder and he wiggled his shoulder continually to keep the strap from slipping off. He had to stop often as the people in front found their compartments and took a while to move out of the way. It was past 11 in the morning but many of the passengers were still lolling in their berths, especially the tired old men and women. Lying amidst their crumpled sheets, with hollow eyes and feet like cracked earth, they were making the most of these hours of enforced rest as the long-haul train from Vishakhapatnam swung through the wide arc of its journey across half the landmass of India.

"Here it is," Vijay announced, sounding relieved that he had found their seats. They drew aside the shabby blue-green cotton curtain and entered the compartment. Berths 7 and 8 were the upper and lower on one side of the four-berth compartment. Lekha's eyes swept over the young couple sitting on the lower berth on the other side. Newly-weds, she thought fleetingly as she and Vijay got down to settling in. They worked efficiently and in sync, quickly stowing away the luggage under the seat and placing the duffel bag and Lekha's backpack on the bunk overhead.

Lekha glanced at Vijay who was looking a bit relaxed now. She knew that her husband suffered from travel anxiety. It was strange that a man who was so cool and unruffled otherwise, had an attack of nerves whenever he had to travel. Whether it was an official trip or a rare holiday, Vijay always got into a blue funk about not being able to make it to the airport on time. It was no different this time, even though this was a rail trip and the station was only 10 minutes from their hotel in Gwalior. This time too Vijay had insisted on arriving early.

"You know we haven't taken a train in years," he had said. "There may be all sorts of issues. We may not be able to wheel our suitcases if there are those footbridges. We may need a coolie. I'd rather be there a bit early because the train stops for only five minutes."

"How early? Two hours?" Lekha asked with a half smile, raising an eyebrow, which she did to great effect when she wanted to be ironical.

Unoffended, Vijay grinned. "It wouldn't be such a bad idea," he said.

Chitralekha Dhar and Vijay Ahluwalia had been married for six years. Both were exactly the same age—34. But Chitralekha, or Lekha, as everyone called her, looked somewhat older than Vijay these days. Her face was beginning to lose its bloom and taking on a slightly wizened look. But she had a trim, youthful figure, with small breasts and flattish hips. Her eyes were bright and piercing, and she had a pronounced jawline which was often thrust a little upwards, as if she had come to know the world too well and had steeled herself to take it on her chin. Her thick, straight hair, which was cut in a boyish crop, had the odd glint of grey. Lekha was yet to decide if she should begin to use one of those magical hair dyes that promised to deliver not just cover for the greys, but also a cascading mass of Aishwarya Rai style glossy brown hair.

Vijay, though, had not changed much from the time the two of them met at the management institute where they had gone to study. He was extraordinarily lanky even now. He was very tall too—over six feet. He had a high intellectual forehead, curly hair (which showed no signs of greying as yet), and a charming smile that belied the shrewdness in his clever, close-set eyes. Both of them were dressed almost identically—in expensive but well-worn branded jeans, T-shirt and sneakers.

Vijay and Lekha had had a B-school romance. They had paired off, like many of their batchmates did. More than physical or emotional chemistry, their mating game had been an exercise in precision planning. It involved examining the choices available, planning the moves and possible counter moves, making a few false starts, and finally zeroing in on the most appropriate candidate, give or take a few minus points. Once they had chosen each other, they had done the 'going steady' routine for the better part of their final year. They were both bright, fiercely competitive and career-oriented, and they were usually given to talking more about their study projects and future plans than about stuff like their undying love for each other. They would have thought that kind of talk was pretty sappy anyway.

When the campus recruiters came calling, and Lekha got a job with an FMCG company in Delhi and Vijay with a consultancy firm in Mumbai – both with a gratifyingly fat pay – their happiness was unblemished by the fact that this would be the end of their romance. They bid each other goodbye, promised to stay in touch, and went their own way.

A few years and a couple of job hops later, they renewed their relationship once again. It was clear that they missed each other. It was clear too, though they never spoke of it, that they weren't about to find the soul mate that they had vaguely wished for. Alone amidst strangers in an unfamiliar city, they reached out to each other with eagerness and relief. They chatted on their BlackBerry messengers every day and once again fell into the habit of confiding in each other.

"Love the comfort level I have with you," wrote Lekha in one of her messages. "It's such a relief to be able to be oneself, you know, to be able to tell someone what an asshole my boss is. And what ass-lickers most of my colleagues are!"

"I'm always there for you, Lekhs, you know that," Vijay messaged back. He unburdened himself to her with no less candour.

They decided to get married because it seemed to be the logical thing to do. It didn't matter that they were not exactly in love. Each knew the other intimately, the habits they had and the hopes they cherished. They had an awful lot in common, and that, they both agreed, was the foundation of a successful relationship. It didn't matter either that they were based in different cities–Lekha was now back in Kolkata and Vijay was in Mumbai. So, notwithstanding the scepticism of their two families who wondered how a long-distance marriage would work, they signed on the dotted line and had a reception apiece in Delhi and Kolkata to celebrate their union. After a brief honeymoon in Mauritius, they got back to their respective work lives. Till one of them found a job in the other's city, they had agreed to fly down and meet each other once every six weeks.

It so happened that Vijay got a break in Kolkata before Lekha managed to find something in Mumbai–which had been the original plan. He wasn't too happy about moving to the city, as he considered it a "non-happening dump where Bongs went mooning about their Rabindranath and their Ray". But he took up the offer of joining an auditing firm as an associate vice-president because it would allow him and Lekha to be together. They got a nice flat on the posher side of Dover Road and finally settled down to a conventional married life, one where they connected with each other every day in the same physical space rather than on Skype or over the phone.

They rarely fought because both were, as they liked to say, "on the same wavelength". Their domestic life was smooth, not least because they had managed to procure an efficient live-in maid who cooked and cleaned for them in return for an exorbitant salary. They put in long hours at work. And when they came home and sat down to dinner, they discussed and dissected their workday in ferocious detail. Their tiredness fell away and they became animated again as they talked about the triumphs they had scored and the slights they had endured. Although, it had to be said that these days Lekha felt that Vijay narrated his victories more often than the pinpricks of his putdowns.

On Saturday nights they went to a club or a lounge with their friends who were quick-eyed, sharp-talking, young corporate types like themselves. Together, they whiled away some hours in a haze of alcohol and thumping music. The music made them shout at each other until they gave up trying to talk and got up to dance on the throbbing floor. When that too began to pall and their jollity collapsed upon them, they shrank from the flashing lights and sank into a stupor on wide settees that were probably made more for making love than for sitting on. They downed their draught beers and margaritas and conversed about pretty banalities that seemed less pretty as the night wore on.

The holiday to Madhya Pradesh had been Lekha's idea. They hadn't taken a break for two years, she pointed out. They were both stressed out, too caught up in the hectic daily grind of their lives. They needed to get away for a bit. Vijay agreed and said that perhaps she was right—they did need some downtime. After some weeks of discussion about whether it should be Kerala, or Thailand, or Madhya Pradesh, as Lekha suggested, they settled on the last.

"Oh, I've always wanted to see the Khajuraho temples! And we shall stay five star," Lekha said happily.

"Doable," Vijay said cautiously. "Five stars in these small towns aren't all that steep. Let's check out the rates." He was careful about money—not stingy, but prudent, he liked to point out to Lekha when she teased him about being a tightwad.

And so they had completed their 10-day trip through Madhya Pradesh and were now on their way back to Delhi. They planned to stay with Vijay's parents for a night and fly back to Kolkata the next day. Both agreed that it had been a good holiday. They had travelled from Khajuraho to Gwalior by car, spending a couple of nights each at Jhansi, Orchha and Shivpuri along the way. They had had time to unwind and discuss some important issues. It was good to be away, they said again and again, though they frequently checked their work mails on their smartphones. They also talked rather a lot about their work, especially whether—and how—Vijay would manage to bamboozle the competition and get into a key division that would give him more visibility. They spoke about whether Lekha's promotion as head of brand, stalled for over a year now, would finally come through this April. "Well, Ashish did assure me that it was a done deal. But you never know with bosses—they'll string you along and then drop you with a thud," Lekha said. "I mean, you've seen Ramanujan! How could he possibly be promoted before me? The man is an idiot! A complete doofus!"

As the train gave a slight lurch and moved off, Lekha looked a bit more closely at the couple sitting opposite them. She had guessed right. They were definitely just-marrieds. The girl had 'new bride' written all over her. Her sindoor was a bit smudged now, but it had been thickly laid in a vivid proclamation of her newly wedded state. The gold locket of her mangalsutra shone like a polished badge, and she sported the telltale columns of red and white bangles that brides in north India wore for a time after their marriage. The bangles rode up almost to her elbows and clattered merrily whenever she moved her hennaed hands tipped with inch-long, hot pink nails.

Lekha put the couple to be somewhere in their mid-20s. The girl was probably a bit younger. She was a thin girl, with a nondescript face and a 'wheatish' complexion. Her long, wavy hair was mussed, and it hung about her like a cloud and looked as if it had just been shaken out of a tightly wound plait. She wore an ill-fitting, flaming orange salwar kurta with an elaborate blue and pink floral embroidery all over its front. From time to time she darted a knowing look at her husband and gave him a mysterious smile. And the man–a tubby, jovial chap with a moon face and hair falling shaggily over his small, fleshy forehead–responded by grinning at her openly and with joy.

Honeymooners! Lekha noted with a mental smile.

The train was gathering speed now. Lekha got up and took out a voluminous thriller that she had been carrying around in her backpack throughout the trip. She still had to get through the last 50-odd pages. She meant to finish the book now. Vijay was already busy reading a copy of a day-old *Economic Times* that he had picked up from the hotel. He made it a point to read at least two business papers a day. Since they weren't always available in the small towns of Madhya Pradesh, he had been mostly looking at them on his phone.

"Really, must you do that even on holiday," Lekha had asked with amused exasperation.

"What's the problem," he said amiably. "Not as if you were talking and I wasn't listening and reading business news instead."

Vijay was such an incorrigible creature of habit, Lekha thought. These days she was no longer sure if she liked that about him. There were simply no surprises about the man. But then she would rather have a solid, dependable husband whose every move could be predicted than some unpredictable lover boy you couldn't count on.

She kept the book unopened on her lap and looked out through the window of the train. Its glass was scratched and opaque with dirt and grime. They had left behind the low buildings and factory sheds of an ugly, semi-urban sprawl, and now the train was hurtling through a scorched scrubland with craggy outcrops of boulders here and there. Distant thatch huts and diminutive humans skidded past. The sun burned through the tinted glass window of the air-conditioned capsule which carried them along and threw an oblong of golden light on Lekha's arm. She touched the window pane with the back of her hand and found that it was warm. It was mid March but the mercury was already nudging 38 degrees Celsius outside.

Well, she wasn't sorry that the holiday was coming to an end. She and Vijay had used the time well. They had had their break and they had taken a very important decision. They had agreed to start a family. The subject had been looming over them for the last one year, casting a shadow on all their discussions about the future. Lekha brought it up almost constantly now. She had broached it tentatively at first. Then, seeing that Vijay was not particularly keen to discuss it, she had kept at it with her usual tenacity.

For Lekha felt that it was time. If she was going to have a baby, she didn't want to put it off any longer. She was going on 35, for god's sake! Vijay, however, seemed loath to give up their hassle-free, double-income-no-kids status, loath to disrupt the smooth amassing of their twin fortune by having a high-maintenance object like a child. So he stalled and played for time, arguing that they should buy a property first. "First a flat, then a baby—that's my plan," he said.

If Lekha was wounded by his reluctance to have a child, she did not dwell on it too much. After all, she couldn't blame Vijay for not wanting to take such an important decision without weighing the pros and cons. So she argued patiently: "We can make a down payment on a flat and still have a child. We are not exactly poor. We can afford a child, if that's what you're worried about."

"My dad was 38 when my older sister was born!" he said stubbornly.

"But your mother was, what, 25?" Lekha countered.

Well, all those silly arguments were thankfully over now that they had taken the DECISION. She was convinced that the timing was perfect. Once she got her promotion, she could afford to slack off for a bit. Vijay too didn't want to change his job just yet. So they were going to remain in Kolkata for the next couple of years at least. Besides, her mother was there in the city. She would be a huge help in the baby care department.

The undeniable rightness of her arguments finally forced Vijay to give in. "Well, okay, logically, perhaps it is a good time," he admitted. He was lying on a lounger by the brilliant blue pool in the hotel in Khajuraho, his eyes unreadable behind his sporty wraparound shades. Lekha sat next to his long, lean, moist body that dried swiftly under the baking sun. A few foreigners were swimming in the pool and a man was lying prone on another lounger, with a floppy hat covering his face and a paperback on his chest.

"Well then, why are you hesitating?" Lekha's voice was low, her sharp, alert face soft, and she bent close to her husband like a beseeching Madonna, though she smelt triumph already.

"All right," Vijay said suddenly, taking off his shades and sitting up.

"Let's do it! Really, let's," he repeated, looking at Lekha and smiling his easy, charming smile.

"Yes!" Lekha exclaimed and did a high five with Vijay like they did when they managed to sell some stocks for a neat profit.

But now that they had decided to go ahead with it, Lekha asked herself if she was happy. Was she truly, sublimely, ecstatically happy about having a child? She had asked herself that question in Orchha after they made their first serious attempt at baby making and Vijay had turned his back to her and fallen asleep at once. They had felt reckless and amorous that evening after drinking a lot of red wine and watching a sound and light show that recalled the loves and exploits of valorous Bundela kings. Perhaps the baby is made already, thought Lekha a little nervously as she listened to Vijay snoring peacefully, as if he did not have a care in the world.

She had got up, slipped on a robe and come out into the balcony of their hotel room. The night was hot and still and there was a dull moon behind the clouds. She could see the shadowy outline of the ramparts of the medieval fort and further beyond, the ghostly spires of the royal cenotaphs where memories of long-dead kings lay entombed. Somewhere there in the blue-black night the river Betwa flowed, gurgling over and around the smooth dark rocks, now gentle, now swift—a live and life-giving force. And in a moment of sudden post-coital self-doubt, Lekha wondered if this was what she had wanted. This even, non-adventure of her life, this meticulous parcelling out of it into must-do stages—education, job, marriage, motherhood, house and so on and on and on. A kind of yearning leapt inside her and she felt a great black hole in the pit of her stomach. Would a baby fill that void, she wondered. Was she missing something? Maybe a baby was not the answer at all. She had come back to bed with fear and disquiet in her heart and had lain awake a long time.

She was thinking about that curious night in Orchha when she was startled by the sound of laughter. She turned away from the window and saw that the newly-weds were laughing. Well, giggling, actually. The thin, brown blanket - standard issue railway bedding – that had been lying in a heap in one corner of their seat now covered the girl almost up to her chin as she sat squeezed against the window. She had pulled her legs off the floor and had tucked them underneath the blanket. Her husband sat close to her, really close, part of the blanket covering his lap, and hanging halfway down his short legs. He had his arm around her front under the blanket and grinned wickedly at her, while she wriggled under his invisible assault, looking at him sideways with a mock frown and a laughing mouth that told him to go on.

Shit, they are making out right here, thought Lekha with a slight shock. She looked at Vijay to see how he was taking this and saw that he had opened his newspaper wide and had disappeared behind it.

That's so like Vijay, Lekha thought with irritation. He was such an awful prude! Why, at Khajuraho he had looked positively pained when the guide was explaining the nuances of the orgy of erotica sculpted on the temple walls. He wore an expression of bored disinterest all through, which Lekha found almost hurtful. This was a dream trip for her. Ever since she had read about Kandariya Mahadeva and the other Khajuraho temples at school, she had wanted to come here and stand before these magnificent sculptures. And here was Vijay spoiling the moment for her by ignoring their exquisite beauty. All because he was a strait-laced stuffed shirt!

She wondered if she should message him now—say something like, "enjoying the free show?" They could have a silent, secret conversation that way just like old times when they conducted their long-distance courtship over BBM. She missed those clunky BlackBerry phones, dammit! They were so much a part of her memory of the sweetness of those days. But it was easy to be romantic online. You could shed your inhibitions and talk of love or lust. Perhaps distance gave you a certain romantic flair, which proximity stamped out.

The couple in front of her, though, were making the most of their proximity. Lekha tried not to look and opened her book to read it. But the giggles and the low, cooing murmur emanating from the other side of the compartment were impossible to ignore. And try as she might, she couldn't help stealing glances at them.

Look at them, Lekha thought indignantly. Pawing each other in full public view! And they were small-towners! Small trader stock, definitely! Well, India was certainly changing! Who would have thought that people like them could indulge in PDA!

And they were getting bolder. The man was planting little kisses on the girl's cheek now, whispering things into her ears that made her bite her lips and tremble with laughter.

How disgusting, Lekha thought, beginning to feel outraged. What a pair of shameless, ill-bred idiots! Well, the girl would soon pop two kids, she thought vengefully, become fat and querulous while the man got busy with his shop or whatever and that would be the end of all this!

And yet, she wondered at this thing they were vibrating with right now. Had they done it on the train last night? Maybe they had had the compartment to themselves. Or maybe not—they seemed not to care either way! And though she scarcely wanted to think about it, she imagined them being at it the whole way, from whichever distant part of the country they were coming from, at it like a pair of joyous young animals, moving as the train moved and the world rolled and pitched with them.

Just then she thought she saw the girl throw her a sly look, as if to say that this moment of power and bliss belonged to her—not to anyone else, and certainly not to this snobby woman with her fashionable haircut and fancy sneakers who was pretending to read a fat English book.

And quick as a flash, Lekha thought, oh, they were showing off! They were flaunting their odious lust, she thought with rising anger, because she and Vijay seemed like a fitting audience. But what had they divined, those two, with their low small-town cunning, their awful primitive instinct?

Minutes later Vijay folded the newspaper noisily and ostentatiously. Then he got up and told her that he was going out of the compartment.

"Need to stretch my legs," he said.

"What time do we reach Delhi," she asked him, looking up at him with bright, pleading eyes, wanting him to stay, wanting to weave a web of conversation which would hold them both in a tight, warm knot.

"About 4.45, I think," he said.

"Do you want to eat now," she asked. "We have those packed lunches from the hotel. I'm quite hungry, actually."

"I'm not," he said curtly. Then he drew the curtain aside and went out.

A little later, an attendant came to take the order for lunch. Lekha did not order anything, but the young man on the other side did. They would take one veg *thaali*, he said, and the two of them would share the food and have it from the same plate.

The girl was talking loudly on her cell phone now, wishing one Sejal Bhabi a "Happy Birday". They had unglued themselves for a bit and one of her salwar-clad legs had emerged from under the blanket. She nosed around with her foot, looking for the glittery golden sandals that were lying face down underneath the seat, wedged between two olive and brown cloth covered suitcases.

"*Hanji, bauh-a-u-t enjoy kiya...*" said the girl.

And the man taking the phone from her a few minutes later reassured the person at the other end: "*Ji, ji, ab tak toh* train time *pey hai. Nahin, nahin, koi nahin. Hum ek aatoo ley lengey.*"

The train was trundling into some big station. People rushed by and coolies ran alongside the train. Some had already materialised inside the coach–thin, wiry men in dirty red uniforms, ducking their heads into compartments to see if there were passengers who needed a hand with their luggage. There was the usual inchoate hum of a busy, overcrowded platform–muffled cries and the echoing boom of the public address system that announced arrivals and departures in short inarticulate bursts; there were ragged vendors, some of them absurdly young lads, who climbed into the train to sell tea, coffee, and packets of potato chips; and there was the heaving mass of people everywhere - sweating, pushing, shoving - all trying to get to their destination or to merely make a living.

Lekha noticed that Vijay was standing on the platform, smoking a cigarette. It must be a long halt then, she thought, or he'd never have had the nerve to step off the train. He looked distant and unfamiliar, like someone she did not know very well. She felt like waving to him. But she did not, lest he failed to see her behind the double glass window and the newly-weds smirked at her useless flailing. She wished she could have gotten off the train too and gone outside where the air was hot and ripe and teeming. But there was the baggage, and she did not want to leave them unattended.

So she sat there as the man and the woman snuggled close once again and went back to their gleeful love play. It was pathetic, pathetic, Lekha thought. And all at once her life was borne upon her on a sheet of smooth, featureless grey. It chilled her heart, but she sat with an expressionless face, her chin thrust slightly forward, and waited for her husband to return.

Do They Have a Merc?

Jyoti missed the exact moment the Mercedes arrived. She had wanted to go with her husband Suresh to the showroom to bring the big silver blue car home. But after days of discussion on how the car was to make its grand entry into the apartment complex where they lived, it was decided that the chauffeur would drive it on its maiden journey and Suresh would accompany him. It wouldn't do for Jyoti to join the party as that would seem, well, a bit too over the top.

"It shouldn't look as though we thought it's a big deal," Suresh said.

"Well, it *is* a big deal," countered Jyoti, who liked to call a spade a spade in the privacy of her home. "Whether people like it or not."

"Sure. But we don't want to give the impression that we think that."

So Jyoti stood by the window in an agony of impatience, waiting for Suresh to show up in their dream car. She drummed her fingers on the windowsill like a hungry bird pecking away at a dry branch. She kept visualising their big Merc moment, when the smooth and splendid machine would glide into their driveway. Would any of the other residents catch a glimpse of it right then, she wondered. Of course, the watchmen and sundry loiterers would gawk, surprised and deferential before it. It would take them a while to figure out that this was now the most expensive car in the building. But that would happen soon enough. And then, when the car sailed in and out every day, folks in the building would surely turn and stare, or perhaps pretend not to have noticed—all the time burning up in jealousy that the Grovers had got themselves a Merc!

Her cell phone began to ring. Thinking it was Suresh, she went scrambling to get it. It took her a while to find her phone because the instrument had a habit of eluding her whenever she was in a hurry to answer its insistent ringing. The call turned out to be from her mother. Jyoti pressed the phone to her ear and ran back to the window. But it was too late. The doorbell buzzed moments later. Jyoti hung up on her mother at once and went to open it.

Suresh stood there, twirling the fat electronic car key around his forefinger. He paused in the doorway for effect, regarding his wife with narrowed eyes and a lopsided smile—every inch the cool dude who's come home bearing an unbelievable prize.

"I mist-eet!" wailed Jyoti, as though she had missed her baby taking its first, glorious, unsteady steps.

When they went out for an inaugural drive that afternoon, Jyoti made Suresh stop the car by the race course. She got out and ran her hands over its cool blue flanks. She caressed its darling bonnet—wide and expansive like a river. She touched the smiley eyes of its gorgeous head lamps, fingered its triumphal three-pointed star, and laughed liked a girl again. Suresh sat behind the wheel with a lazy-smug expression on his face, watching his wife stroke the car like a new lover.

Weeks before, Jyoti had carefully examined a Mercedes CLA Class car in the showroom. She paid no attention to Suresh who was deep in conversation with a young saleswoman dressed in a tight-fitting shirt and trousers. He stood with his stomach sucked in and his legs wide apart in an inverted V because he felt that made him look slim and rakish and not flabby-middle-aged as he really was. It was a posture he was wont to adopt from time to time, especially if young women happened to be in the vicinity. Jyoti thought this was unutterably foolish of her husband, but after so many years of marriage, she allowed him his small pleasures. So she ignored Suresh and concentrated on the car. She didn't understand much about cars—she didn't even drive one, for that matter. But she understood stuff like looks and status, and she thought this one was a winner on both counts. "I think this is it," she said after a while, interrupting her husband's earnest tête-à-tête with the young woman in the too-tight shirt.

At which Suresh shrugged extravagantly at the sales woman and smiled like a zillionaire about to buy a bauble for his wife.

"Well, what can I say? The lady has made up her mind."

Actually, they had both made up their minds quite sometime back.

When Suresh got the go-ahead from his company to upgrade his sedan to a bigger and pricier one, Jyoti had a brainwave.

"Let's get a Mercedes!" she said.

"Oh, imposs," said Suresh, goggling at her audacity. "It costs how much—30 lakhs at least? More, probably. The company would never pay for it."

"We could pay the difference."

"There'd be a lot to pay," Suresh said dubiously.

But the idea took hold. They kept coming back to it like a pair of work bees who had found a secret hoard of godly nectar. It was sweet and potent even to talk about. And the more they talked about it, the more fascinating it seemed. They stayed up late into the night to discuss it, they pondered it during their morning constitutionals. They continued the delicious debate even when Suresh was on tour and Jyoti called to give him lengthy updates on Mercedes Benz models and their prices. They worked out the finances and the EMIs until every impediment had been looked at and overcome–at least on paper. They had come to agree that it would indeed be something if they managed to pull it off. It would show the world that they had arrived. They had bought a flat in a leafy, upscale neighbourhood in Kolkata, they had sent their only son to the US to study for his graduate degree. Suresh had recently become the CFO of his company and they had paid a fortune to acquire an exquisite little Manjit Bawa sometime back. A Mercedes would sum it all up brilliantly. It would be, to use Jyoti's favourite expression, the cherry on the cake. Besides, a Merc had a certain mystique, she said. It was a symbol of luxury, it was all about being in a class apart. She sounded a bit like a breathless promotional for Daimler AG as she sang its praises, but in point of fact, Jyoti could be anything when it came to bludgeoning the competition. She had devoted years and years of her married life to this–channelling her energy and intelligence to the realisation of their common cause. She had achieved nothing personally. But that had long ceased to bother her. Helping Suresh along in this relentless and unending climb up the slippery pole was her greatest achievement. She was a pro at the job and could seize the salient points of a scenario like this one with the cut glass clarity of her mind.

The bottomline, as Jyoti put it succinctly, was that although everyone they fraternised with had big cars (they wouldn't be friends with people who didn't), no one had a Merc.

"You know Bunny Bose–he's got several super luxury cars, including a Ferrari and a Porsche. Someone told me he recently bought a Jag as well," Suresh said.

"Yes, but we don't really know Bunny Bose, do we? I mean, it's not as if we socialise with him. We just keep hearing about him and his phenomenal wealth and his big fat cars. What does it matter what he has or x, y, zee has? The point is, does anybody we know have a Mercedes?"

She rolled her tongue around the word and pronounced it elegantly, pausing between the syllables so that it sounded mysterious and foreign, like a connoisseur's fine wine. "Mer-say-des," she exhaled, and gently corrected her husband each time he said "Mercydizz". Jyoti was proud of her convent education and disdained the 'Indian' accents of her circle of friends. And Suresh, though given to striking his legs-wide-apart superhero stance before strange young women, deferred to his wife's superior knowledge in this as in many other matters.

"Mer-say-des," he repeated after her obediently. "No, people we know certainly don't have it."

Which, of course, was the whole point.

They completed the spin around the race course, looping back through Casurina Avenue and on to the Strand. To their right, the river grinned broadly in the bright afternoon sun. Wispy white clouds flitted across a fabulous blue pottery sky. To Jyoti the whole world looked happy today. Suresh drove slowly, reverentially, and the car cruised along.

Let's go to the club," Jyoti said.

"Now?"

"Yes. Why not?"

"Okay," Suresh said and changed gears.

They had both known all along that they would head to the

club after a drive in their new car. In any case, they went there on Saturdays and Sundays and hung out with their friends Arun, Tina, Dhruv and Anju. Sometimes a few others joined in—the singleton Yatish, or even the uppity Sanjeev and his second wife Yasmin, who held themselves a bit aloof from the rest because Sanjeev, who was not yet 40, had already become a director of the company where he worked. When the prospect of buying a Mercedes was beginning to look real, the first thing Suresh said was, "They'll be totally blown away!"

"Who," Jyoti asked, knowing who he meant, but wanting to hear it all the same.

"Oh, Arun, Dhruv and all,"

"I know," Jyoti said softly, and pushed out her mouth in a tight, ruminative smirk like someone who has got the sweet foretaste of victory in a long imagined showdown.

At the club, Suresh parked the car carefully and they both got out. They walked towards the gravel-laid grounds where people sat in clusters around wobbly wooden tables covered in green gingham tablecloth, shooting the breeze and downing beers or sipping tea. Beyond them the golf course stretched out like an emerald sea, rolling away into the golden haze of the afternoon. They spotted their friends and waved.

Dhruv waved back, "Hey, Jo, Surie, you're late, guys," he shouted over the clamour of voices.

Jyoti quickened her pace. She couldn't wait to tell the others. But careful now, she said to herself. She must choose the right moment for maximum effect. She didn't want that gleaming piece of silver blue bombshell to get lost in the silly vortex of everyday conversation. On the other hand, they had both decided not to appear too excited about their big news. It was going to be a tricky manoeuvre. She only hoped that Suresh wouldn't blurt it out like an over enthusiastic schoolboy. No, she would do the talking, as they had decided. She would choose her moment and then–oh, what fun, she thought, shimmying along, skimming the joyous air that smelt of grass and shone like a thousand suns.

They reached the table amidst a symphony of ha-ais and helloes. Two more chairs were dragged in and Jyoti and Suresh sat down.

"What took you so long, *yaar*? I thought we could play some doubles tennis today," Dhruv said. "Anju here has been waiting impatiently."

"Sorry, didn't get my racquet along," said Suresh. "Let's play tomorrow?"

"Nope, can't make it. Am off to New Jersey tomorrow night," Dhruv said, seeming to grow a little more, seeming to fill up the chair. "Have to pack, you know."

"Oh, right, you did mention."

"Dhruv is certainly going places, hunh," Arun said, shaking his head appreciatively. He spoke with a slightly nasal American accent, probably because he was the one who got to visit the US most often on work. Then, turning to his wife, who was a wiry woman dressed in a short tee and bermudas, he said, "Tina, tell Jo and Surie your big noose."

Jyoti swivelled towards Tina sharply. What big news? What? *What*? shrieked her mind. Tina crossed her trim legs, blew out her cheeks and said with a shrug, "Well, I clocked 10 km on the treadmill today."

"Oh, wow," Jyoti said, hating her.

"Hats off, *yaar*," said Suresh appreciatively and with that air of universal benevolence which almost never left his face.

They all went to the gym in fits and starts. They were all pushing 50—an age when the conversation often swung to matters of fitness and health. They had resolved to work out at the gym when they visited the club. But barring Tina, none had kept at it seriously. Tina had beavered away on the machine, no one had known quite how diligently. And there she was today—the queen of the treadmill—sitting amidst them like a star with an arrogant tilt to her head, her short hair slick after her post-workout bath, swigging bottled water and telling Jyoti and Suresh about her slow, hard climb to the 10 km milestone.

"I work up the speed gradually. Start right at the bottom—at 2.5 kmph and then work my way up to 6 kmph, by which time I am running, of course. You should try it, Jo," Tina said, looking pointedly at the neat roll of fat around Jyoti's middle that never went away no matter how little she ate. "It'll work wonders, I guarantee it. You'll feel great. Energised. You just have to be a bit disciplined. It's all in the mind," she said and tapped her temple.

This was too much, thought Jyoti, barely able to conceal her anger. What was Tina making such a big deal about? Bragging about 10 kilometers! It was nothing! Nothing compared to ... compared to... And all at once, she forgot the elaborate tableau of announcement she had planned. "Folks, we have some news too!" she said abruptly and immediately felt something warm and wonderful suffuse her whole being. She threw a quick smile at Suresh's direction, who was smiling too, and plunged ahead, "We've just bought a Merc!"

"What!"

"Muck?"

"Wow, really?"

"Merc—as in a Mercedes?"

"Yes, a Mer-say-des," Jyoti said triumphantly, beaming broadly and demolishing the treadmill and its pitiful foot soldier with one swift blow.

"How come?"

"Well, done, may-an," said Arun, shaking Suresh by the hand.

"Wow, Jo, that's so fantastic, *yaa*! And you didn't even give us an inkling," Anju exclaimed, looking a little hurt that her friends could be so secretive about their plans. "And we tell you guys everything!"

"A Merc!" Tina managed to utter through waves of hysteric laughter. "You won't believe what I heard at first—I heard 'muck'!"

A hundred questions followed, which Suresh and Jyoti answered patiently and at times, mendaciously.

"Oh, we didn't buy it," Jyoti said. "It was his office. They insisted, you know, now that he is the CFO and all. Anyway, it's really just a CLA class," she said, trying to sound off-hand and modest.

"Oh, it's just a poor CLA Class," Dhruv said, crinkling his eyes and mimicking Jyoti. "But seriously, this is great news!"

"Have you told your son?" Arun asked.

"Yeah, we were on FaceTime with him a few days back and told him about it," said Suresh. "He was thrilled!"

This too was strictly untrue. Far from being thrilled, their 19-year-old son, who was studying in Pittsburgh, had been shocked at this fresh evidence of how unbelievably old-fashioned his parents were.

"Aw, Mom, Dad, a Merc is so yesterday! There are a 100 other cars you could have gone for that're much more trendy. If a Beamer was too expensive, why didn't you go for a Volvo or something? A Merc is so completely boring! I wish you'd asked me about it."

It had dimmed their joy just for a moment. But they bounced back almost immediately, laughing at their son's reaction and shaking their heads approvingly at his contrariness.

"He has to be different! That's just like Buban!"

But though they didn't admit it even to themselves, their son had struck a discordant note. It was as if the first stone had been cast upon their idea of pure, 24-carat happiness. And they feared to tell their friends about his reaction lest they too went after it with sticks and stones.

When the afternoon spilt and drained into a slow, uncertain dusk and the fairway emptied of the last straggling golfers, they were still sitting around the table, dealing banter and bonhomie, keeping up the merriment lest something like envy showed through.

"Drinks in honour of the Merc," Arun shouted and the others slapped the table and said, "Hear, hear!"

"Don't worry, you won't get off with just a round of drinks," Anju said archly, rolling her eyes. "Hey, Jo, how about a party for the Merc?"

"Yes, yes, a coming out pharrty for the Mercedes! Come on, Surie, how about it, may-an?"

"Guys, it's no big deal," Suresh protested.

"Really, it isn't," Jyoti said, smiling and sipping a fresh lime and soda. "It's no big deal," she repeated, feeling sated and generous like a boxer who has landed a knockout punch and, for a bit, is at peace with the world.

"By the way, just remembered, you know Keshav Sabharwal?" Arun queried.

"*Hanh, hanh, woh* Williamson Russell *wala*?"

"Yeah, that's the one. He's also got himself an ultra luxury car. I met him and his wife the other day."

"Do they have a Merc?" The question shot out of Jyoti before she could stop it. She looked away in embarrassment, wondering what that sounded like (Aggressive? Childish? Pathetic?) and aware of four pairs of eyes glinting at her, picking up her gaffe and storing it away for a hilarious dissection later.

"No sweetie, sorry to disappoint, but he's actually done one better," Arun said, reaching out and squeezing Jyoti's hand. "He's bought an Audi Q5!"

"Really? He's filthy rich, or what?" said Tina.

"Yup. Tea gardens in the Dooars. Family's loaded. Of course, he's not as loaded as Bunny Bose. You know Bunny Bose—he's got a whole fleet of those babies. Ferrari, Porsche, a vintage Rolls-Royce Phantom—you name it, he's got it."

Jyoti and Suresh exchanged an imperceptible look, as if to say—how boring and predictable of them to bring up Bunny Bose! Who cares about him anyway?

"Hey, but I'm still impressed with Surie here," said Dhruv. "He's done it without a family fortune, *yaar*! We humble Korean and Japanese car owners are honoured to be in such exalted company! We grovel before thee," he said and bowed his head low in a gesture of obeisance.

They chortled madly at this and Suresh ordered one more round of beers.

Soon, another couple joined the group. Sanjeev and Yasmin floated towards them, pulled up two more chairs, and sat down. Sanjeev was a keen golfer and he tended to talk rather a lot about the game.

"Awhh," he sighed, dropping into the chair with a thud. "I've had an excellent round today! Got birdies on the seventh and ninth holes—can you believe that?"

"Wow, terrific," Arun said, "Are you playing at the tournament next month?"

"Let's see. I mean to."

"You must," said his wife Yasmin. "It's amazing how good he's gotten and how fast," she said, looking around and frowning in puzzlement and pride.

"Mm, need to work on my drive, though," said Sanjeev.

"Speaking of drives, guess what champ here is driving these days," said Dhruv. "A Mercedes!"

"*Achha*? Which class did you buy?" Sanjeev asked. "Hey, we don't care which class. We're just happy that classy couple Jo and Surie are giving a pharrty for the Merc," said Arun.

"Really," Yasmin raised one brow and looked at Suresh with a quizzical smile as though she had never heard a more ridiculous thing.

"What nonsense! Of course, we aren't," Jyoti said quickly, forcing a laugh. She did not like Yasmin at all. First, the woman was way too busty. Second, she had once caught Suresh making a fool of himself with her at a party. He had had one too many all right, but the slut with the oversized udders must have led him on.

"*Arrey*, you know, I read somewhere that Ludhiana has the highest concentration of Mercs in India," Sanjeev said. "Apparently, it's the favourite car of filthy rich farmers. Helicopter weddings and Mercs in the stable along with *asli* Jersey cows—that's what they swear by."

"That's so funny," Tina giggled. "Is it true? Jo, next you'll have to organise a helicopter wedding for Buban!"

"Never heard that one before. I thought those farmers preferred Audis, actually," said Suresh, his expression of perennial benevolence slipping just a little.

"Well, I've certainly never come across this piece of news anywhere," Jyoti tittered. "But it's a nice story. It's probably an urban legend."

"Is that what's called an urban legend? I thought an urban legend was..."

A little later, all of them trooped towards the car park to have a look at the Mercedes. It was evening now and the sky was a deep purple, illuminated here and there by blobs of artificial light alive with their diadem of minute, shivering insects. The Mercedes wasn't immediately visible in the shadows. Then Suresh pointed it out to them. They went near to examine it, almost as if they wanted to make sure that the afternoon wasn't misspent talking about something that did not exist at all.

"Awesome!" Dhruv breathed.

"It's a beaut, may-an," said Arun.

"Too cool," remarked someone else.

"My brother has a BMW," Yasmin declared suddenly.

"Yeah, I drove it on the Bombay-Pune expressway last month," said Sanjeev. What power the car has! Uff, totally blew me away. Now, if I had the money, that's the car I'd like to buy."

Jyoti and Suresh got into their car. They waved as the others stood and watched the Mercedes swing noiselessly around and depart like a vanishing moonbeam.

The moment they were out of sight, Jyoti undid her smile. "Did you hear that rubbish about Ludhiana," she exclaimed angrily. "Such utter rubbish! I'm sure he made it up then and there! And BMW, my foot! How come she never mentioned it before? How come she remembered it the moment she saw our car? And I didn't like the way Arun said, 'How much money are you making?' What on earth was he trying to say?"

"They'll all change their cars now, you wait and watch," Suresh said softly.

Then they drove back home in silence.

Mrs Sharma

I met Mrs Sharma a few weeks after moving into my new flat on Rowland Road. It was a two-bedroom apartment, and much bigger than what I needed. But I took it because it belonged to a cousin who had offered it to me at a throwaway rent. He wanted someone "known and easy to oust" to stay there, he joked. I wanted a decent place to live in—so the matter was settled right away.

The building had some 20 flats. There was a little quadrangle in front of it where cars drew up, and at the gate a couple of thin men in uniform masqueraded as security guards, chatting and arguing loudly. The building's children played here in the evenings, weaving in and out between the cars. I had seen Mrs Sharma—though I didn't know her name then—lean over the wrought iron railing of her balcony and call out to her son, asking him to come up. She stayed on the floor below mine and I could see her wide balcony, which was packed with potted plants, from the window of my living room. I had often spotted her tending to her plants and giving instructions to the *mali* in a low voice.

She was a fair, buxom woman with brownish, shoulder length hair that was usually tied in a pony tail. When I saw her in the mornings, she was invariably dressed in a faded blue or peach-coloured sleeveless nightie that revealed her chunky upper arms and dimpled elbows and probably made her look plumper than she was. Once or twice she had looked up suddenly, as people being watched often will, and our eyes had met. But she did not seem to take offence that I was watching her. She smiled at me and I smiled back.

I had settled down at my new digs. I had decorated the living room with some hastily bought furniture. My mother offered to do up the flat for me. But after staying on my own in Delhi for three years, I had got used to doing things my way.

It was Diwali when I met Mrs Sharma formally. I had come back from work early that day. I had bought two boxes of *diyas* and meant to light them and put them out on my window ledges. It was early evening and you could already hear the crackers going off–both the deafening big bangs and the staccato gunfire kind that sputtered on for several seconds. It sounded as if the city was under siege and was being bombarded from all sides. I lit my *diyas* and was watching their flickering blades of flame when the doorbell rang. It was the lady from downstairs.

"Happy Diwali," she wished me, smiling shyly.

"I am Mrs Sharma. I live in 2B," she said, pointing downwards. She was carrying a plate of sweets and savouries, which she was now proffering to me. I was new in the building, no, she queried rhetorically, so she thought she'd come by and say hello. I was nonplussed for a moment. Then I wished her back, introduced myself, and invited her in. She gave me a timid smile and said, "All right. Just for five minutes."

Mrs Sharma seemed quite transformed from her shiftless morning self. She was wearing a scarlet salwar kameez in a flowing silky material that made a swishing sound when she moved. Her spangled dupatta was drawn demurely over her heavy bosom and she wore gold *jhumkas* in her ears and some gold bangles as well. She had a sallow complexion, large brown eyes, and a broad, friendly mouth that was wont to break into a slow, diffident smile. She was anywhere between her mid to late 30s, and though her face had softened and spread, she was pretty in a comfortable, matronly way. I thought she would have looked prettier still had it not been for her restless brown eyes that seemed unable to focus anywhere for too long, as if she were distracted by too many things at once.

Mrs Sharma looked around and complimented me on my living room.

"Did you buy the flat," she asked straightaway.

"No, er, it belongs to my cousin. I have taken it on rent."

"Good, good. It's looking very nice. The previous tenants, the Chakrabartys, they used to keep the place like a pig sty, you know. Your cousin must have heaved a sigh of relief when they moved out."

I smiled and said apologetically, "I'm sorry, I have no sweets in the house to offer you."

"Oh, that's all right," she said, waving her hand as if to forgive my woeful lack of resources as a host. "You live alone, you go out to work, how will you get the time to do all this?"

I made coffee for both of us and with some embarrassment asked her if she would care to have some salted cashews and potato chips–about the only snacky stuff I had in stock.

She smiled. "Oh, just coffee is fine."

Mrs Sharma proceeded to ask me about myself. She looked impressed when I told her that I was a journalist, and was utterly confounded to learn that though my parents were right here in the city, I had chosen to live on my own. I was single, of a marriageable age, and Mrs Sharma was of the view that girls like me had no business living alone when they didn't have to.

"You are spoiling your chances of a good match," she said with such sincerity and concern in her voice that I didn't have the heart to laugh.

She told me about herself too. Her husband was in the plywood business and they had been married for 14 years. It was a love marriage, she said with evident pride. She had been his secretary and he had fallen in love with her and married her against his family's wishes. Her son Aman—an overweight kid whom I had often seen downstairs charging around like a demented bull—was 11.

"He is too naughty," she said, crinkling her brows. "Manoj—that's my husband—is very lenient with him. I tell him to be a bit strict, but he spoils him. He is the apple of his eye, you know."

Mrs Sharma stayed for nearly an hour that evening. She was talkative and gossipy in a mild, good-natured way. She filled me in on my neighbours—the Kampanis in 5C who had been raided by the income tax department, the Mukherjees in 3A who had an autistic son, the Duttas who had been stevedores once upon a time, and someone else who had just lost his wife to a sudden heart attack. She was talking about people I didn't know and couldn't put faces to, so I wasn't terribly interested. However, I appreciated her wanting to include me in the social circle of the building. This was her way of making me feel at home here, and I decided that I quite liked her.

"Call me Indrani," she said, touching my arm when she took her leave. "And please do come over sometime."

I didn't get around to doing that much. But over the next few months, Mrs Sharma—I never got used to calling her Indrani either—often dropped in. If I was back home early, and she saw lights in my flat, she would sometimes drop in for a chat. She was keen to know exactly what I did in the newspaper. She often flipped through my magazines and examined my books and read their titles. She told me that she used to write poetry once. But they were never any good, she said sadly. Sometimes she came to give me a bowl of something she had cooked that day–*gajar ka halwa* or a chocolate pudding, or some new recipe of chicken biryani that she had tried. I wondered if her early attempts at poetry had been as dismal as her attempts at cooking. For there were occasions when I carefully flushed the stuff down the toilet lest my maid got wind of it in the morning and relayed my dastardly act of betrayal to her.

I soon found out that I wasn't the only creature Mrs Sharma liked to feed. She also fed stray cats, which was probably why there were so many of them lurking around the building all the time. Every afternoon she took whatever scraps and leftovers she had and went down to give it to the cats. They were sleek and cunning and they watched her coolly till she came up to them and then got busy with her offering. If she was late, they went up the stairs and scratched impatiently at her door, letting off a terrific meowing for their daily benefit meal.

Almost a year went by. I was now on nodding terms with most people in the building. I knew who was who. No doubt they knew all about me too, thanks to Mrs Sharma and, of course, my help Malati who jobbed in several flats and was a wondrous fount of information. My friendship with Mrs Sharma had not progressed beyond a certain point, though. She and I did not really have much in common, and after she had told me all there was to tell about her life and the residents of the building, even her mostly one-sided conversations began to be throw up long pauses in between.

There was another reason I wasn't as comfortable with Mrs Sharma as I had been in the early days. I had taken a violent dislike to her husband, and found it hard to conceal my irritation when she spoke of him fondly.

I had seen the man a couple of times when I came back from work late in the night. Once, when I got out of the office car which was dropping me home, I saw him stagger unsteadily towards the lift. Suddenly, he turned and looked at me. His expression was so unspeakably offensive, so obviously loaded with meaning, as if to imply that he knew what I had been up to at that late hour, that I fell back to let him go on ahead. His physical appearance was equally repulsive. He was tallish, with a wizened, ape-like face, a bald head and a broad flat nose. He had a sparse moustache, a gross snout of a mouth, and he carried a small paunch on his otherwise thin frame. He stared insolently at me with his beady eyes till the cage of the lift shut him in. Maybe I was tired and overwrought that night, but I felt that I had seen something frighteningly evil, something that could barely be described as human.

I found out who he was the next morning. As usual, Malati, my help, enlightened me. He was none other than Mr Sharma. I learnt that he came home very drunk every night, often in the small hours of the morning. He was known to beat his wife, and she had been seen with a black eye and swollen lips and bruises on her arms sometimes. On each occasion, she claimed lamely that she had slipped and fallen in the bathroom.

"But who's she fooling," sniffed my maid. "They have no relation–those two! The husband treats her like dirt. Everybody knows that."

I was immensely sorry for Mrs Sharma. I was angry for her too. I wondered if I should ask her about it sometime, but I didn't want to appear nosey and interfering. I thought I'd look an awful fool if Mrs Sharma acted astonished and offended. Certainly, she had never betrayed the slightest hint of unhappiness or trauma to me. On the contrary, she always seemed to be the epitome of the contented housewife, given to prattling about her household and maid problems and her son's exams and gently bragging about her husband's loving, giving nature.

"You must wish me belated happy birthday," she told me playfully when I bumped into her in the lift one morning. (Which, naturally, I did at once). "You'll never guess what Manoj got me! He bought me a diamond ring–an absolute rock! I'll wear it and come over one day," she said, pursing her lips with barely contained delight while her anxious brown eyes flitted hither and thither.

Or at another time: "Manoj has bagged a huge contract, you know. He's said he'll put aside an amount for Aman's higher education right now. Do you think an FD of 50 lakhs would be enough–you know, for when he is 21–if he wants to study management or go abroad and all?"

And so on.

It made me wonder if I had been paying too much attention to servants' gossip and if everything was fine with Mrs Sharma after all. But each time I thought of her husband's leering, bestial face, his drunken yells to open the gate at one or two in the morning, I was ready to believe the worst. As time passed, I began to feel that perhaps Mrs Sharma had sought me out because I was a newcomer in the building and hence unaware of the kind of life she really had. Perhaps she had thought that the pretty fiction she spun about herself could be played to me safely, that where others would curl their lips in ridicule, I, who was a stranger, would believe her make-believe that she was a loved and cherished woman. I can't say I wasn't struck by how poignant her act was, or from what depths of misery it arose. But my sympathy for her slowly gave way to annoyance when she kept up her radiant tales of an idyllic household. Really, I thought indignantly, she ought to realise that after so many months I wasn't likely to be taken in by them.

Perhaps Mrs Sharma had sensed the change in my attitude to her. For she rarely came over now. Then one day, she appeared at my door fairly late in the evening. I had a few friends over for dinner, and there was a lot of talk and laughter going on. Mrs Sharma stood at the door and spoke in a low voice. She seemed to be in a state of great agitation. She said that she was sorry to intrude, but it was an emergency and she didn't know whom to go to. Her troubled brown eyes refused to meet mine, and she kept twisting her hands wretchedly. Concerned, I asked her what the matter was.

"I need some money urgently. I am really, really embarrassed to ask you. Tomorrow is the last date for paying Aman's quarterly school fees. And Manoj forgot to give me the money before he went out of town. I don't know what to do!"

I asked her how much she needed.

"I'm short by 7,000 rupees," she said in a despairing, almost inaudible voice.

I told her not to worry. I had about Rs 5000-odd in the house. I said I'd give her that and pop across to the ATM tomorrow and get her the rest.

"Oh, thank you, thank you," she said, almost in tears. "I'll return it the moment Manoj gets back."

The next morning I went to give her the money. Mrs Sharma, clad in her usual shabby nightie, seemed speechless with emotion and gratitude. Her face puckered up and she looked as if she were about to cry.

"I am so sorry to impose on you," she whispered.

"Don't be silly–it's nothing," I said, embarrassed, and left quickly.

I had felt like asking her if she didn't have any money at her disposal at all. Surely she ought to have at least a joint account with her husband and an ATM card? But these were delicate questions and I feared asking them mainly because of the uncomfortable answers they might elicit. My sense of outrage and shock at the abusive marriage she seemed to be trapped in had plateaued into a shrugging acknowledgement of her situation. It was not an unusual story, after all. And while I wanted to help Mrs Sharma, who had been good to me in her warm, big-sisterly way, at the end of the day, I didn't want to get involved in other people's troubles. I was a city dweller, fully fledged and thoroughbred, and I knew how to pick my blinkered way through the ugliness and squalor all round.

It wasn't until about three weeks later that Mrs Sharma returned the money to me with many thank yous and profuse apologies for the delay. She told me some more tall tales about how her husband was caught up in a business deal in Assam and had returned only the day before. I listened patiently and wondered if she knew that I knew she was lying. Everyone in the building had heard the awful ruckus the week before when a very drunk Mr Sharma came back home late in the night. He had let fly the choicest Hindi invectives and had slapped one of the watchmen for not opening the gate fast enough when he honked. I heard later that the guard had quit, threatening to avenge the insult that had been done to him. The matter had led to an 'emergency meeting' of the building committee to which Mr Sharma had been summoned.

He did not show up, of course, so everyone carried on about his unacceptable behaviour for some time, then fell to arguing about how much money was needed to paint the building, and finally dispersed in heated little groups, having accomplished nothing.

I began to consciously avoid Mrs Sharma after the second time she asked me for a loan. On this occasion, she looked much less distraught. She hurried over her story—something about having dropped a lot of cash from her handbag and being reluctant to ask Mr Sharma for more money when he was having a little trouble in his business.

"But I'll pay you back, *pakka*. In a week, I promise," she said and smiled a tired, nervous smile.

I gave her the 10,000 rupees she asked for, but promised myself that I would have to decline the next time she came around with a similar tale. I didn't doubt that she needed the money. Her scumbag of a husband was probably not giving her enough to run the house. But it wasn't my problem. I couldn't go on lending money to Mrs Sharma—what if she were unable to pay me back? I would have to put my foot down, I decided.

As it happens, she did return the money fairly quickly. I was relieved. Still, the next few times I saw her, I let my eyes skim past her as if I had not noticed her. I felt like a bit of a heel about it, but it was self-preservation, I told myself. She couldn't treat me like a bloody ATM just because she had plied me with her lousy cooking!

Mrs Sharma did not come by again. In fact, I hardly ever ran into her anymore. I even stopped looking out at her balcony lest she saw me and smiled and we fell into an uncomfortable neighbourly communion.

Weeks flew by. I was busy with my own preoccupations. I was under some pressure at work. I had been put in charge of a department and my subordinates were doing their best to stonewall my efforts to prove myself in my new position. Mrs Sharma and her odious husband lay almost forgotten, when one day, my maid Malati–that bringer of a thousand half-true tidings–gave me the latest on her.

"Do you know what your friend did yesterday?"

"Which friend?"

"2B, 2B-ee," she clarified, her eyes dancing.

"Oh yes, what about her," I asked.

Mrs Sharma, Malati said, had gone on a rampage the previous afternoon. People in the building had suddenly heard an almighty crash, followed by several others in quick succession. A great hullabaloo ensued in the quadrangle below, and people rushed out to see what was happening. Mrs Sharma was seen throwing out her potted plants. She lifted them one by one and casually dropped them over her balcony railing while everyone skipped out of harm's way and shouted at her, asking her what on earth she was doing. Smelling a sensation, some ladies in the building went and rang her doorbell. But a calm and stone-faced Mrs Sharma neither answered the door, and nor did she stop until she had thrown out each and every one of those plants and completed the meticulous destruction of her beloved terrace garden.

"She's gone mad, totally mad!" Malati pronounced. "It took them hours to clean up the mess!"

I was shocked. So Mrs Sharma was having a breakdown! Well, with a husband like that, it was a wonder that she did not have one earlier. For some reason, though, I felt a twinge of guilt. She was not my responsibility, certainly not, but she had been in pain and I had chosen to ignore her. And, suddenly, that bothered me.

Meanwhile, Malati had more information to share: "And here her husband has been complaining about thefts in the flat. Go see, I'm sure she's the one who had something to do with it!"

"What thefts?"

"God knows! Apparently some valuable things went missing from their house. I think they did it themselves, and they're blaming the servants now. And have you seen her lately? She looks like a skeleton! I tell you she's gone bonkers!"

I went over to my living room window and looked down at her balcony. And true enough, all her carefully tended plants had disappeared. The spreading areca palms, the masses of ferns, the rubber tree that had grown so sturdy and tall, and even the yellow hibiscus plant that burst into startlingly brilliant flowers—they were all gone now. The balcony that she called her 'green oasis' lay empty—a scooped out, shell of a place ringed with reddish brown stains where the pots had stood and scattered with loose earth here and there. All that remained was a solitary dishcloth that hung from a sagging clothesline and trembled in the hot morning air.

I made up my mind to go and see Mrs Sharma. It was the least I could do, I thought. But it wasn't until a few days later that I managed to return from work early enough to pay a visit to her. She opened the door herself and looked surprised to see me. Then she smiled a ghost of her old, sweet smile and asked me to come in.

Malati had been right. Mrs Sharma looked like she had been on a crash diet. All her cheerful chubbiness had vanished. Her face was gaunt and it had the greyish pallor of one who has been sick a long time. She was dressed in her blue nightie and it hung loose on her shrunken frame. I was struck by how unadorned and bony her wrists were, and how prominently the trellis of veins stood out on the back of her small, neat hands.

When I went inside, I was in for another shock. Her once crowded drawing room was empty like an abandoned play-field. The statues and the lamps, the slightly tacky brass and wooden artefacts, and the pictures on the walls seemed to have been spirited away somewhere. Only the bare bones of some furniture stood by like poor props in a sombre theatre. It was as though Mrs Sharma had decided to do away with all that she valued in one catastrophic sweep, until she was left with nothing–nothing but her own faded person in her faded blue shift dress.

I sat gingerly on the edge of the sofa, feeling awkward and unsure about where to begin.

"Are you going away somewhere," I asked finally, gesturing to the denuded room that lay in semi darkness, lit only by a single naked bulb on a twin bracket lamp.

"No, No. Nothing like that," she said.

"I heard you were ill. So I came to see you."

"I was...a little...yes. But I am on medicines now. Manoj brought a doctor over. I am much better now. See, I lost so much weight! I always wanted to lose some weight. It's happened at last," she said, smiling a little.

Then she got up abruptly and went to another room where the television was blaring away. She said something to her son. The boy gave a retort in a shrill, high-pitched voice. And Mrs Sharma came out like a whipped dog, shutting the door behind her.

"I want to put Aman in a boarding school," she told me in a matter-of-fact voice, coming back to sit down opposite me. "He is getting too naughty for words."

We sat in silence. The overhead fan spun at breakneck speed and a little ball of hair danced about the dusty, unswept floor. In that half light the room seemed vast and formless, its edges lost in strange, dark shadows. Mrs Sharma sat with her hands folded on her lap, her head slightly tilted to one side. She seemed to be contemplating the shadows, contemplating the emptiness washing over and around her, lost to the world, lost in herself, lost, above all, in the unfathomable tumult of her own meltdown.

After a while I said desperately, "Mrs Sharma, if you need any help, if there's anything I can do..."

She floated up from somewhere and turned her wasted face to me. "I need a job. Can you get me a job," she whispered. "I need a job right away. We are having some money problems, you see," she said and spread out her hands to indicate the bare room and the vanished bric-a-brac. "What am I supposed to do if there is not enough money? Manoj was very angry. But what was I to do?"

I thought of her husband's nightly drinking binges. The money problems did not seem to have put a stop to those, I thought grimly. But I could not tell Mrs Sharma that. For there she was, touching my arm with her light, spidery fingers and looking at me beseechingly with her hunted brown eyes. "You know a lot of people. You can get me a job. I need the money! I have to run the house...I have to send my son away from this, this...!"

I asked her if she could not go away to her parents' house with her son.

"You need to get away. You need some rest."

Mrs Sharma shook her head. "It's not possible. My parents... no, I have nowhere to go."

And then once again she spoke, the words coming faster and faster now: "Anything, I'll do anything. I used to be a good secretary. I can pick up computers...I know I can..."

Over the next few months I asked several people for a job for Mrs Sharma. She was a college dropout, but she knew secretarial work, or, at least, had known it once upon a time. She had a nice disposition. I was sure she could be a good secretary if she brushed up her skills a little. I did manage to get her interviews in a few places.

But for some reason, they did not work out.

"You tried," she comforted me when I expressed anger at the inexplicable behaviour of people who needed secretaries. "It's difficult at my age. I have to accept that."

The good thing was that she seemed to have got over her illness. She had lost that hollow, haggard look and spoke normally enough. I had expected her to borrow money from me again, and had vowed that I would not refuse it. (At least, not for sometime.) But she did not. Maybe the good Mr Sharma was fulfilling his duties as a husband and father, I thought. Perhaps their domestic arrangement, no matter how flawed, was back on an even keel.

Soon after this, I went away for a holiday in the UK. I had decided to spend a month with a friend who lived in London. I had had a more or less amicable parting of ways with my boyfriend of two years. Yet the experience had left me with an aftertaste of regret. I thought backpacking around England would be a good way of putting the useless episode out of my mind.

On the very first night of my return to Calcutta, I bumped into Mrs Sharma. I was on a late night flight back to the city, and it was nearly 3 in the morning when an Uber deposited me in front of my building. Right then, a big cherry red sedan drew up. I saw Mrs Sharma alight from it.

I was astounded to see the change in her. She was dressed smartly in a cream and gold *kalidar* kurta and churidar ensemble which showed off her heavy breasts and flattered her now slimmer figure. She wore very high gold stilettos, carried a matching gold clutch, and her hair, which was left open, seemed a richer shade of brown than I had known it to be. She wore quite a lot of makeup too and her sweet and gentle mouth was drawn in flaming, voluptuous lines. She looked sexy and confident and her eyes shone when she saw me.

I waved at her as I wheeled my suitcase in. I was glad to see that she was getting about.

"Good to see you, Mrs Sharma," I said. "Been out partying?"

"Good to see you too," she said, smiling broadly. "So how was your trip?"

And before I could reply, she continued breathlessly, "No, no, no party! Guess what? I've got a job!"

"Really? That's wonderful!" I exclaimed, genuinely pleased. "Where are you working?"

She told me that she was working in a call centre and that she was enjoying the work. "Manoj got me the job," she said, almost preening in delight. The only problem was that the hours were bad, she said with a mock grimace. Sometimes she had to go to work in the afternoon and sometimes she had to do night shifts. But she always got a drop back. And the money was good. And her bosses were pleased with her. In fact, she could soon be made a team leader.

"I just love it," she said rapturously. "It's a wonderful atmosphere there and the people are so nice. I never knew a call centre could be so wonderful!" she said, making it sound like a mini heaven, a workplace utopia, where bosses were always kind and appreciative and every colleague was a helpful friend.

I smiled at her enthusiasm. The enthusiasm of a newbie, I thought with amusement.

Then we squeezed into the lift—me with my suitcase and bags of "duty free" and the bright and bedecked Mrs Sharma, tottering a little on her four-inch heels. I thought I smelt alcohol on her breath. Mixed with her stale perfume, it gave off a sour odour that lingered like a bad taste in my mouth.

I woke up late the next morning. Malati arrived, and we got busy with cleaning the flat which had been shut for more than a month. In between the dusting and the cleaning, Malati said conversationally, "And have you heard about the 2B madam? These days she goes out every night all dressed to kill. Says she's got a job. Now who's she fooling, you tell me?"

The Party

Sheelu was making chicken sandwiches. She was proud of her chicken sandwiches and thought she made them rather well. She carefully cut the crusts of the slices of bread with her long, sharp kitchen knife. Then she softened the butter and spread it on the bread. A dash of mustard, a lashing of mayonnaise—"and there goes the chicken now," she said aloud, placing the bits of cooked chicken on the open faces of the bread slices. She finished the sandwiches after sprinkling them with salt and pepper, and then cut them diagonally with the deftness of a surgeon wielding a scalpel.

There, that's done, she said to herself, arranging the sandwiches on her white gold-rimmed bone china platter. She surveyed them contentedly. They looked so perfect, she thought, the soft white triangular shapes lying there like a spray of perfectly symmetrical flowers.

There were 16 sandwiches, which would be quite enough. After all, there would be only five people coming to tea. Six, if she included herself. And maybe little Rohan, her niece Lali's three-year-old son. Besides, she had made an aloo chaat. She had bought baby samosas from a neighbourhood savoury shop. She had also baked a pineapple cake, which was one of her culinary triumphs, people said. And she had the dosa batter all ready. She would serve her guests freshly fried dosas. That ought to be a treat too.

Of course, people didn't throw tea parties these days—not for adults, that is. Her friend Mona had hooted with laughter when she invited her. "Tea," she exclaimed. "Gosh, Sheelu, that's so bleddy Victorian! Why not a dinner," she demanded.

"Well, I thought let me have a tea party for a change. It has some novelty, you have to grant that," Sheelu had replied defensively.

She had not told Mona that a tea party would be much less expensive than a dinner, though she did not doubt that Mona, shrewd as she was, had known the reason right away. It couldn't be helped, Sheelu thought, shrugging. She was damned if she was going to have more than two formal dinners a year. A school teacher's salary did not allow her too many indulgences, but she still made it a point to have two fairly elaborate dinner parties every year. One took place on her birthday in August. Many of her friends and relatives landed up to wish her anyway, so she had been making a party of it for many years now. The other dinner was the really special one, held in honour of her brother Ronojoy, her dear Ronnie, when he paid his annual visit to Kolkata in January.

This was a one-off. Her favourite niece Lali and her American husband Charles were in town. It was the first time they were coming to India after their wedding five years ago. So Sheelu felt she simply had to have a little 'do' for them. She and Lali used to be really close once. They used to be like sisters. Despite their six-year age difference, they had shared an uncommon intimacy.

But face it, Sheelu thought, they had very little in common now. At 42, her life had settled into a dull groove. She was a prim school teacher doing her best to hold on to the frayed apparatus of her elite upbringing. When she stopped to think about her life, which was often, Sheelu realised that there was a certain finality about it already. The gorgeous, unpredictable drama of life belonged to others. She was the spectator—others the participants in that play.

Lali's life, on the other hand, seemed full and fecund and alive with possibilities. She was married to a nice looking American man, they were well off, and she had a three-year-old son too. She had seen pictures of little Rohan at Lali's mother's house. The child had Lali's eyes—big, round and questing. Lali had given up her job in a publishing house to bring up Rohan. She supposed Lali was up to her eye balls in domestic bliss.

When Sheelu heard that Lali was coming with her family she had made up her mind to call her over. She knew they would meet at the houses of some of their innumerable relatives. They would be falling all over themselves to invite her and her American husband. There would be many lavish dinners—'slavish' is what she liked to call them. People had a habit of showering hospitality on friends and relatives who lived abroad. It was an unspoken quid pro quo. Wine them and dine them in India and then, when you've mustered enough cash or air mileage points for a holiday in the US or the UK or wherever, they would have to return the favour and put you up for a few days.

Well, *she* didn't need to cosy up to people with an eye on a foreign holiday. Her brother Ronnie had been asking her to visit the US for years. He had even told her that he would send her a ticket. No, her invitation to Lali was completely without self-interest. She was doing it for old times' sake. Maybe a part of her wished to reignite their friendship and repair their splintered camaraderie. Maybe she felt a little guilty about the way she had acted with her the last time. It was the time of her wedding to Charles. Sheelu hardly spoke to Lali then, and when she did, she spoke with ill grace.

It was nearly five o'clock. Time for her guests to arrive, Sheelu thought. She was scrupulously punctual herself, and she detested the fact that most people made it a point to turn up late at parties. How ludicrous people were–everyone vying with each other to arrive late to show that they were too busy or important to make it on time! But such were the hazards of calling people over, Sheelu murmured to herself, as she looked around to see if she had forgotten anything.

Her living room always looked charming in a muted, old world sort of a way. Today, it had been dressed up a little more. She had placed a vase of pale yellow gladioli on the occasional table in the corner and a bowl of blood red roses on the baby grand piano which she still played occasionally. There were bits of crystal here and there–a Swarovski swan, a Murano dolphin–and some finely wrought china figurines her father had got from Dresden when she was a child. The dining table had been covered with her heirloom white lace table cloth. It was dull and creamy with age, but looked what it was–rare and delicate. She had brought out her best china too–her mother's treasured gold rimmed tea service. The silver candelabra and cake dish were out as well. It had been quite a job to get them polished. She had tipped the *mali* a good 50 rupees when he brought them back to their gleaming splendour. They shone softly now in the dead light of the fading sun.

Sheelu switched on all the lights. At once the room flamed up at her, its quiet elegance charged with a kind of brazen life. The wine red Murano dolphin flashed, the Swarovski swan swam in a prism of light, and the silver candelabra glinted hard and bright.

Sheelu stood blinking slightly. Was there too much light here, she wondered. And would she look too old and withered in this hot shower of light? She often worried that her features were settling into the contours of a permanently disapproving school marm. Her skin, once smooth as honey, looked patchy and spotted now. And that tight, sour smile—how did she come to have it? People used to call her attractive once. Sheelu and Lali are the two beauties of the Chatterjee family, they used to say. Boys found her tall shapely body, her sharp features and full mouth sexy. She had many admirers—boys from good families who her parents approved of. Boys with a "future", as they put it. They had hoped that Sheelu would choose one of them. But she chose Ajitesh, the struggling artist, who didn't have a penny to his name.

Her parents had been shocked. "It's madness," her father had told her. "You'll always be comfortably off, I'll see to that, but will it be honourable for your husband to live on your income?"

"Of course, he won't live off me, Baba. We won't get married until and unless he starts selling his paintings."

"Well, then, be prepared to stay unmarried. I've seen his paintings. They are perfectly vile," her father had said.

After a few years, though, Ajitesh did begin to sell his paintings. Critics began to notice his work and talked appreciatively of his dark realism and his brooding depiction of ugliness, which, they said, was eloquently transformed into beauty. Their verdict seemed a bit confusing, but Sheelu didn't care. She was ecstatic at his success, overjoyed that her faith in him had been rewarded. For years and years she had made Ajitesh her *tapasya*, her one transcendent goal. She had gathered up her passion, will and energy and laid them at his altar. And finally her prayers had been answered. Ajitesh was on his way to fame. Her only regret was that her parents did not live to see that he had made it.

But then Ajitesh did the unthinkable. He broke off their engagement all of a sudden.

"Sheelu Mashi, is it true," Lali had asked her with shocked indignation when she came to Kolkata for her wedding. They had met in between her whirlwind trousseau shopping. How beautiful Lali had looked then, thought Sheelu. She was radiant, talking fast and excitedly. Gosh, she looks like she's won a lottery, Sheelu had thought and then scolded herself for being catty and resentful. Naturally, Lali was happy. She of all people should not begrudge Lali this moment of happiness. And Lali was not like her other nosey relatives. There had been real concern in her voice when she had asked her about her break-up with Ajitesh.

"What happened? You must tell me everything. Okay, we'll talk later," she had whispered amidst the gaggle of relatives milling around.

They did talk later, but Sheelu felt that Lali was distracted, and that she didn't really care to hear about the story of a break-up when she herself was so thrilled about her wedding.

Still, Sheelu told her what everyone seemed to know already. She told her that Ajitesh had come to her one day and said that he had fallen in love with another woman. But she did not tell Lali how his words had struck her like lightning, charring and twisting her forever.

The doorbell rang. Ranu, the elderly maid, went to answer it and Mona swept in like a mini tornado, singing "Hello, hello" as she came inside, and rushing to envelop Sheelu in a hug. Sheelu returned the hug and then extricated herself, smiling. Mona, a large, rotund woman, who could be embarrassingly direct at times, was dressed in a black and gold kurta and palazzo pants today. It made her look a bit like a caparisoned drum, Sheelu thought affectionately. As if she had read her mind, Mona asked, "How do you like my dress?" Then, without waiting for Sheelu's reply, she went straight to the table, "Where's the food," she asked. "What all have you made?"

"Nothing much. Just some chicken sandwiches and aloo chat. I've baked a pineapple cake, got some stuff from Haldiram, and I'll make dosas."

"I remember Lali used to love your pineapple cake,"

"And my chicken sandwiches," Sheelu nodded, smiling.

"God, all this talk of food makes me hungry. When are they coming?"

"Well, I said 5 o'clock to all of you," replied Sheelu tartly.

"Sorry, Sheelu," Mona said, grinning. "I know you get mad if people land up late. But don't be such a school teacher, *yaar*–I was only 15 minutes late. That's not so bad."

Mona was Sheelu's childhood friend and knew most of her family well. Her husband was posted in Chennai now. She had not joined him there because her daughter was in senior school and they did not want her to change schools at this stage. But Mona was wont to tell people breezily, "Frankly, I wouldn't have moved to Chennai even if there had been no school issue. Who wants to leave Cal? This is the best city in the world! And setting up house all over again? Catch me doing it!"

Mona let her considerable bulk drop heavily into the sofa. It protested with a squeak and Sheelu winced. Mona really oughtn't to do that, she thought. She was quite sure that the springs in her big green armchair had collapsed because her friend chose to sit on it so often.

Sheelu's cousin Ranjan and his wife Namita were the next to arrive. Ranjan seemed to have become stouter since she had met him last. He was sweating profusely even though it was late autumn and the weather was pleasant and cool. His face too seemed larger than she remembered and it had the slightly flushed look of someone who drank too much and too often. His wife Namita was a petite woman, with neat, regular features and a thin, superior smile.

The moment they came in, Ranjan began to boom. "You're lucky you caught me in town, Sheelu," he said. "I'm off again tomorrow."

"Really, he's hardly ever in town," Namita said, making a proud-aggrieved face

"So, no drinks, eh," exclaimed Ranjan. "That's the beauty of having people over for tea, ha ha..."

"Rawn-jone..." said Namita, trying to sound reproachful.

Sheelu smiled calmly and said, "Oh, but please, do help yourself–I have some good whiskey...there's the Beefeater gin too that Ronnie brought for me the last time."

"No, no, just joking, *baba.* Wifey here thinks I drink too much anyway!"

Then, settling into the sofa comfortably, Ranjan turned his attention to Mona.

"So how are you, Mona. Long time no see. Your husband is still with International Agro? I met their MD the other day. Great guy. His uncle was the director of ICI...my father knew him, in fact..."

Without looking at Mona to see how she was taking this, Sheelu muttered an "excuse me" and escaped to the kitchen.

She took a quick look at everything. Her maid, who had been with the family for two decades, sat drowsing in one corner. She did not rouse her. She tasted the aloo chat again. Today's was not one of her best. Too little salt? Not enough tamarind sauce? It had seemed all right when she made it. But now she found it flat and tasting faintly of tannin.

She suddenly felt very tired. She had been keyed up about this party. She had been thinking too much about it. She was glad it would be over soon.

"Gosh, it's nearing six. Where are Lali and Charles," she said, coming back into the living room.

"Maybe they are still jet-lagged," Namita offered.

"Of course not," said Mona briskly. "Didn't you say they arrived five days ago," she asked Sheelu.

"Yes. Well, perhaps I should call and find out.

Just then the doorbell rang. "There," they all cried out together. Sheelu went quickly to the door. It was Lali...her slender, elfin face alight.

"Sheelu Mashi! So good to see you," Lali said and they embraced fondly.

"But where is Charles? And Rohan? I was hoping you'd bring him along too."

"Oh, Rohan has a slight tummy upset. And Charles ran into a friend who is touring India. He decided to show him a bit of Kolkata. He sends his apologies and says he will come and see you next week."

"Oh," said Sheelu, disappointed. But she noted with pleasure that Lali hadn't acquired an American accent even now. She had lost quite a bit of weight, though. Always slender, she now looked waif-like in her Fabindia churidar kurta and her bright eyes seemed over large on her pale, chiselled face.

"What a shame," Mona said. "We were really looking forward to getting to know our American *jamai*."

"I know! I am sorry," Lali said with a comical grimace, going up to Mona and hugging her too. "But you'll meet him soon, I promise!"

The greetings went on. "Good to see you Ronju Mama. And

Namita, wow, you look just the same! And how are the boys? They must be quite grown up now?"

"The older one is in Class IX. He won a science competition recently," Ranjan said proudly.

"Wow, really?"

"*Achcha*, sit, sit," Sheelu said. "Let's hear all your news, Lali.

"Well, nothing much to report, really. I'm a full-time wife and mother. Rohan keeps me on my toes. I'm trying to teach him to speak Bangla."

"Are you? That's so creditable," Mona said.

"How old is he now," Namita asked.

"Three and a half. Wait, let me show you some snaps."

Lali took out her phone and touched open a picture folder. They crowded dutifully around her to see the pictures as she swiped them one by one. There was Lali and Rohan playing on a bit of green in front of their house; Charles flat on his back, holding up his laughing son; Lali and Charles, looking at each other and laughing as lovers will; Rohan perched on the roof of a low slung olive green car—his pudgy arms reaching out for something and Lali holding him and grinning broadly into the camera...

On and on came the pictures, one perfect frozen moment after another. They all made appreciative little noises—saying how adorable Rohan was, how beautiful their home was, how nice Charles was looking, and how Lali was positively blooming. And Lali, smiling all the while, continued with the slightly breathless commentary of her bliss. "Here, this is Rohan's second birthday party, this was when we went to Martha's Vineyard—Charles has a friend who has a house there, Rohan and me in the neighbourhood park..."

Sheelu sat on the arm of the sofa. She leaned in over the others' heads and watched the slide show unfold. She couldn't see very clearly from where she was, but enough to make out that one joyous snapshot of Lali's life was melding into another until it all became a hazy, triumphal march under her eternally moving forefinger. While the others oohed and aahed, Sheelu struggled to hold on to her polite interested smile. Oh lord, how long would this go on, she thought exasperatedly. Had Lali lost her mind? Was she going to show them all the photographs they had ever taken? How...how...crass! How utterly embarrassing! Didn't Lali realise what a fool she was making of herself! How could she be so insensitive...how could she be such a bore!

She couldn't bear this ridiculous exhibition one moment longer, Sheelu thought. And she cut in sharply now, "Well, if this is going to be tea, I had better serve it fast. Otherwise it will soon be time for dinner."

Lali stopped at once. She looked up at Sheelu, smiled, and switched away the pictures. "Oh yes, I mustn't be such a bore and swamp you with all these photos," she exclaimed.

Everyone protested and said they loved the pictures and wanted to see some more. Sheelu stood embarrassed and nonplussed for a moment. Then she fled into the kitchen, shouting behind her, "*Aei* Lali, I want to see the snaps properly later. I could hardly see the screen with all you guys crowding around!"

She felt her face burn with shame. That was churlish, churlish, she told herself. She sounded so harsh! So sarcastic and bitter! And oh, what were they going to think now? What would Lali think? She felt naked, exposed, stripped of the sheltering mask she wore every day. This party was a terrible idea, she thought miserably, and busied herself with the task of serving the food and getting it over with as soon as possible.

So now the platter of chicken sandwiches, which had been kept covered with a napkin, was carried out. The baby samosas and the aloo chaat were put on the table too. She placed the pineapple cake on her silver cake dish fringed with roses and tiny cherubs. The silver candelabra that held the six red candles were lit. The food was nothing much but it was laid out in style.

Lali came up to the table. "Wow. This I love!" she grinned. "Your chicken sandwiches and pineapple cake! Some things never change. Sheelu Mashi, remember how you used to say I'd never learn to cook? Well, what do you know, I have learnt to bake a mean pecan pie! Actually, Charles's mother taught me—his parents are southerners, you know. If you come to New York, I promise to make you the best pecan pie on the east coast!"

"But you can't live on pecan pie, my dear," Mona said. "Hope you can make some basic stuff—*dal, bhaat, maachh, mangsho*."

"Of course, I can," Lali said laughing. "Whoever visits shall not starve. That's a promise!"

"*Achha* listen, y'all start helping yourselves," Sheelu said. "I'll fry the dosas and serve them hot. And then we can have the tea."

"I'll come and help," Lali said.

"No, you won't," Sheelu said firmly. "You just sit there and relax. It won't take me long."

She went into the kitchen again. The maid was beating the dosa batter as instructed. Sheelu lit the hob, smeared a large skillet with a little oil, and began to fry the dosas.

She dropped a big blob of the batter and spread it around evenly—so the crepe would be thin and crisp. Mona wandered in to see how she was doing. "I can't for the life of me understand why you do this when dosas are available outside," she said rolling her eyes. "Why bother?"

"But I like making them myself, Mona. And you have to serve dosas straight off the fire. What's the fun of having cold, limp dosas?"

"Well, darling, you could've ordered something else then! But you're a glutton for punishment. Okay, I'll take this one," she said, picking up a folded dosa. She took a bite and gave a thumbs up. "Great, as usual. You really should've got married and had a bunch of kids whom you could stuff to your heart's content."

"That is what I call a politically incorrect remark directed at an old maid," Sheelu smiled.

"Come on, I'm your oldest friend! I can say it," Mona retorted and waddled out.

Sheelu went on frying the dosas. She spread the creamy batter round and round and watched it bubble up and turn golden and crisp. She suddenly had a vision of herself frying dosas ten, fifteen, twenty years later. Her relatives, her grand nieces and nephews would say, "No one can make dosas the way Sheelu does." And she? What would she feel to see her life distilled into the even golden brown of a perfectly turned dosa?

"Came to see you making dosas," said Lali, walking into the kitchen.

"Come come," Sheelu said brightly, conscious of an embarrassing moistness in her eyes. Oh, what an unmitigated disaster this evening was! She hoped Lali was not looking at her too intently. "Take this one, and some chutney too," she said, thankful that her voice sounded normal.

Lali put a bit of the dosa into her mouth. "Delicious," she exclaimed. "You're missing all the fun in the living room, by the way. Ronju Mama's just been boasting about his father-in-law's house in north Calcutta. 'It's mammoth,' he kept repeating. 'Built over 10 cottahs of land. They even had a small zoo once upon a time,' etc etc."

"He's such a idiot," Sheelu said, making a face.

"But listen to what Mona*di* said. She told him that her husband's company has given him a 3500 square feet flat in Chennai's Boat Club Road."

Sheelu laughed. "Wasn't he shattered?"

"You bet. He looked aghast. 'But that's a very premium area,' he muttered in a hushed voice. I can tell you, Mona*di* has really gone up in his estimation. He is now doing the sum, figuring out how much it would cost to buy a flat like that."

They both burst out laughing. "He's insane!" Sheelu said, feeling as if she and Lali had been transported back to the time when they made fun of the same people and sprinted along the same sunny path of life.

"It's good to be back," Lali said, munching on her dosa. Sheelu looked at her and smiled.

After a few minutes, Lali said in a low voice, "Sheelu Mashi, my marriage is over."

"What!"

"Yes...Nobody knows it yet. It's kind of awkward to tell your parents this when you've come for a holiday with husband and child in tow," Lali said expressionlessly. "It's...it's weird...I never knew you could go on being normal and yet feel so completely hollow and wretched inside."

Her words fell into the silence of the kitchen like small, hard pebbles. Sheelu listened to their dull clatter and quite forgot about the dosa on the fire. "But...but...why?" she stammered. "I mean... the pictures...What happened?"

Lali shrugged and continued in a flat monotone, "Old story. He's having an affair with a colleague. A Colombian girl. She's just 25. I found out recently. He says it was a mistake. But it's been going on for months. A mistake he kept repeating for months! I could have left him right then. But there is Rohan. The trip to India was all planned. I didn't want to cancel it. Strangely, he did not want to either. And I need time to think. I have to figure things out...I didn't plan to tell you really, but I felt I'd go crazy if I didn't tell someone...I thought you'd understand..."

Sheelu felt tears streaming down her face. Her own unshed grief rose up from the dark dungeon of her soul, and it came out in a rush, came on and on, washing over her as the dosa hissed on the smoking skillet and slowly burned and burned.

Daddy is Home

When the rains finally came, Charu was beside himself with delight.

"Ma, Ma," he called out to his mother and did a little jig. "Look, it's raining! What fun!"

Nandini looked at her son and smiled.

"Well, it won't be much fun when there's water-logging on the roads. You might get late for school. There will be traffic jams... Have you thought of that?"

This dampened Charu's enthusiasm somewhat because he didn't like to be late for school. Waves of anxiety rose inside him if he was late for anything. Traffic jams were double trouble—they made you late, and they made you feel as if the air around you were slowly draining away. He felt physically sick whenever they got stuck in Delhi's intractable jams. When he was younger he cried. Now, he quietly suffered his violent unease.

But this was Saturday morning. A school day, with or without traffic jams, seemed very far away. And here was the rain coming down in a mighty whoosh, drenching the leaves on the trees and drumming on the dry, dusty earth. He could already smell that first-rain scent, redolent of the earth, redolent of something edible and vaguely delicious.

He went out into the balcony and stood there, holding the railing with both hands, throwing back his head and arching his thin little body like a bow. The rain slanted into him, wetting his upturned face, his head, his arms. The park in front of their house was ghostly in the rain. Charu closed his eyes and imagined its sun-blasted ground sucking up the downpour. Happiness bubbled inside him. The park! It would soon be green! In a few weeks the grass would grow back and the bare brown patches would be gone! And best of all, the hibiscus sapling he had planted would flower soon! He chuckled softly at the thought and looked up at the roaring shower, marvelling at the way it came down from some mysterious place in the sky where, Ma said, the gods lived.

"Charu, please come inside," Nandini called out. "You're getting all wet. You'll catch a cold."

The sound of the rain muffled her voice. But Charu could guess what his mother was saying. When he pretended not to have heard, Nandini came out into the balcony to take him back inside. And Charu, his wet face glistening, his large, nut brown eyes shining, turned and hugged her. He buried his face in the folds of her swaying skirt and inhaled her sweet, lemony fragrance. "Please, Ma, let's see the rain for a bit longer," he whispered with something akin to ecstasy.

A few minutes later, Nandini gently led him away. "That's enough getting wet in the rain, Babu. Go change your clothes and get ready. It's nearly 12," she said and shut the glass door to the balcony.

Charu went to his room to take off his rain-spattered shirt and change into another. Bashonti, their household help, came to help him. "I can manage," Charu told her with polite firmness. Bashonti sighed and said, "Such a small boy and such attitude already! Okay, okay, I'm going!"

Bashonti was a stout, middle aged woman. She had taken care of Charu since he was a baby. Nandini called her her 'rock'. She was a Bengali like Nandini and it was thanks to her that Charu had learnt to speak his mother tongue. Nandini and Charu's father Ananth, who was from Tamil Nadu, both spoke to him mostly in English. It was part of Parenting 101 in upper middle class urban India–if you had a child you spoke to him or her almost exclusively in English. The odd vernacular phrase did crop up now and then, but on the whole, whether it was baby talk or discipline, parents avoided using Bengali or any other Indian language in their conversations with their children. The journey to be a global citizen began from the crib.

Charu was fond of Bashonti Mashi. She made him yummy aloo pakoras and *payesh* too, which he loved. But he didn't want her fussing around all the time. He was seven, wasn't he? Almost seven and a half. He certainly didn't need her help to put on his clothes.

He changed quickly and was out of the room in a trice. Nikhil would be here any minute. They were to go out with him for lunch. Later, they would go to the airport to pick up his dad. Charu had been looking forward to the lunch because they were going to his favourite restaurant in Khan Market which made the best chocolate sundaes in the whole world. The chocolate was thick and sweet and nutty. It was like slurping up chilled liquid Snickers. Besides, going out with Nikhil was always fun. He called him Nikhil, even though he was really Nikhil Uncle, his father's best friend from his engineering college days. But one day, Nikhil had said to him, "Hey Charu boy, let's drop the uncle thing, hunh?" He sat down on his heels, put his hands on Charu's shoulders and said to him in that glowing voice of his, "Just call me Nikhil, okay?"

"Why," Charu had asked seriously. He had been taught to add an 'Uncle' or 'Auntie' to the name of every adult he knew. It was the mark of their superior status vis-a-vis children like him. Nikhil's voluntary abdication of authority baffled him.

"It's because we are friends–so no uncle shuncle between us," Nikhil had said, smiling his big, goofy smile.

Charu liked Nikhil a lot. He cracked jokes. He was also a good mimic and could do Sachin Tendulkar's soft, papery voice perfectly. He had taught him to play Monopoly, a game none of his classmates knew, and had taken him to see Disney movies a couple of times. Best of all, he knew how to do magic. He could make a coin disappear. One moment it lay round and shining in his hand and the very next, he made it vanish. He waved his hands about, said abracadabra, and produced it from under his armpit. Then he sniffed it and made a face. This made Charu laugh uncontrollably. He never tired of this trick and often asked Nikhil to do it.

"Okey-dokey, here it comes–the one and only magic show for the benefit of the one and only Mr Charusudan Ramakrishnan," Nikhil would announce in a loud, dramatic voice. When he was younger, Charu clapped his hands at this. He didn't do that anymore, but the trick was still a treat. He knew his mother enjoyed it too. She bent her head slightly and pursed her lips in a tight, smiley pout. Sometimes she reached for Charu's hand and gave it a little squeeze. It was like a pact between the three of them. A magical pact.

His father Ananth didn't think much of Nikhil's magic. "Nikhil is such a juvenile," Ananth said, shaking his head. "The guy needs to grow up!"

That's how Charu had learnt the word 'juvenile'. Ju-ve-nile-ju-ve-nile-ju-ve-nile-ju-ve-nile–he repeated it to himself several times after Nandini had explained its meaning to him. Then he strode around the house, reciting it like a marching mantra, his arms pumping, his heels striking the floor hard in the manner of those splendidly dressed soldiers whom he had seen on TV during the Republic Day parade.

Ananth was away setting up a power plant in the interiors of Andhra Pradesh. He had been gone for more than a year, but Charu didn't miss him at all. He visited Delhi once every two or three months. Besides, they were often on Skype. In the evenings after Nandini came back home from the office of the NGO where she worked, Charu sometimes asked her straight off if they would speak to Papa today. If she said, "Um, maybe not today," he secretly rejoiced. He disliked these video chats with his father. Papa sat on a dining chair in a room with pale blue walls. His laptop was on the table in front of him. There was a dull strip of fluorescent light on the wall. Papa sat with his back to the light, his face shadowy, his expression hard to read. When he brought his darkened face close to the screen, it looked huge and scary—like the face of a giant.

Sometimes he asked Charu what he had learnt at school today. If he said he hadn't learnt anything new, Papa was quiet for a few seconds. Then he said cheerfully, "Oh, that's all right, you can't be learning something new every single day!"

If he knew that, thought Charu, why did he ask?

Once, when he was told to go play because Papa and Ma wanted to do some grown-up talk, he lingered outside the door long enough to hear him say, "Nandini, is he coping? Or is he falling back? He seems strangely sullen, unwilling to talk about his school or his lessons."

"What do you mean, coping? And sullen? He loves going to school," Nandini exclaimed indignantly. "His assessments are always good! He's a happy, bright, sensitive child! If you grill him like that, obviously he'll go silent!"

They had an argument after that. Charu could have stayed on to listen some more. But he didn't because it was very tiresome. His parents argued often. Even over Skype. They used to argue earlier too, before his father left for the power plant work. They lowered their voices if they thought he was within earshot. But that didn't fool him. At night their fierce, low-pitched words funnelled into his sleep. Sometimes he woke up and heard the whispers of his dreams come alive in the other room. He heard fragments of words. Angry. Bitter. Sarcastic. When there was silence at last, Charu lay awake, his mouth dry, his heart jerking near his throat. And as he lay clutching his worn blue satin side pillow, he was filled with dread that Nandini would get up and tiptoe into the night, never to be seen again.

It had stopped raining. The day had opened up like a flower—glorious in its post-shower loveliness. The sun was out, the leaves alight, and the texture of the world cool and silken. But their afternoon plans had been abandoned. Nikhil had called Nandini a little while back to say that there was some water-logging in parts of south Delhi. It was decided, therefore, that instead of having lunch out, Nikhil would come over and they would order food in.

Charu was disappointed. He had been looking forward to going out. What was the fun of eating restaurant food sitting in the house?

When Nikhil arrived, he went to him and asked,

"Lots of water-logging?"

"Oh, no. Just some bits here and there, because it was such a sharp shower. But Khan Market is a long way off. And then we have to go pick up your dad. We don't want to get stuck somewhere and get late, right?"

"But what about the route to the airport," Nandini asked, looking worried.

"It'll clear up by then," Nikhil said airily. "His flight lands at 5, no?"

"4.50, yes. Well, I hope you're right. Charu, you better not come along. He really does fret when we get stuck in a jam."

"You're worrying unnecessarily, Nandini. It should be totally fine by then," Nikhil said. "It's not even raining anymore."

"No, I want to go," Charu said with as much firmness as he could muster. Nikhil always drove them to the airport to pick up Papa, and Charu loved the ride. Besides, Nikhil stocked Lays chips in the car. That was an added attraction. Ma *never* bought him chips. She said it was 'junk food' and bad for him. Strange that whatever Ma called 'junk food' was so good to eat.

Their lunch had been delivered in round white plastic containers. Nikhil was very fond of 'Bong' food so Nandini had ordered from a Bengali restaurant in the neighbourhood. There was *mochar chop, luchi, chholar dal, ileesh bhapa* and steamed rice. Bashonti set the table, and watching her shake the mats with a mighty whup before placing them, Charu realised that she too was upset that they hadn't gone out. For it was only when Bashonti Mashi was displeased that she made a great deal of noise while going about her work. It was her code for I'm-angry-so-don't-mess-with-me. His mother simply avoided speaking to her when she was in one of her *bartan*-banging moods.

Nandini and Nikhil ate slowly. They were discussing a book she was reading. Then Nikhil started talking about his boss who,

Charu gathered, was a funny man. Nikhil called him 'watanajjob'. The way he said it and laughed every time, Charu could make out that it was a word for a funny man.

He ate one *luchi* and a bit of the *chholar dal*. Then he poked around the fish and its profusion of fine bones and made a pretence of eating a little. Nandini, always jollier when Nikhil was around, did not seem to notice. So he asked her if he could help himself to some of the chocolate ice cream kept in the freezer.

"You haven't finished your food, Charu," Nandini said. "Honestly, this child doesn't want to eat anything. Just look at him, getting skinnier by the day. I don't know what to do with him!"

"I'm full," Charu said earnestly. "May I have three scoops of the ice cream?"

"Three!" Nandini exclaimed and rolled her eyes at him.

"Hey, let him," Nikhil said, laughing. "If not now, when? When he's 40?"

Nandini smiled. "Okay, just this once. But only because we missed the lunch out, hmm?"

Charu wandered off to the balcony with his bowl of ice cream. He had made Bashonti Mashi shake out some Hershey's chocolate syrup into it too. It tasted good–though not nearly as good as that chocolate sundae he would have had at the restaurant. He ate the ice cream with concentration, swirling it around his tongue, letting its coldness warm up just a little before allowing it to slither down his throat. Out there in the park, Rakesh and Bunny were already setting up the wickets. The ground looked slushy but nobody minded that! Sometimes Charu joined them in their five-over matches. But everybody said he was a lousy batsman because he always got out quickly. Sadly, he wasn't a good bowler either.

His father had got him admitted to a tennis academy last winter, probably because he had realised that Charu wasn't much good at cricket. But he hated it there. The coach made him hit the ball against a wall for hours. It was dull and boring, and after a month, he had refused to go anymore.

"Okay, if you don't want to play tennis, fine. How about badminton then? Or swimming," Ananth asked him when he came to Delhi a few weeks later.

Charu shook his head and looked away.

Ananth spread his hands in a gesture of irritated disbelief. He was a sports buff and had played first division hockey at college. Charu's lack of enthusiasm for sports was almost like a personal affront, as if the boy were denying his genes. He turned to Nandini and said, "You know, at this rate he's going to become a sissy! He doesn't like any games, for god's sake! My son, and he doesn't like sports! I can't believe it!"

"Stop pushing him, Ananth," Nandini retorted. "Let him discover what he likes. The heavens won't fall if he doesn't play games. Maybe he is not the sporty type. Not everyone is made the same way! Maybe he will be an artist. Or a poet."

"Yeah. Sure. Or maybe he'll just be an effeminate, namby pamby mama's boy!"

"Will you stop?"

Charu had listened to his parents bickering over him. He looked from one to the other and back again, as they lobbed their anger at each other. Then he went to his room, took out a Spider-Man comic book and started reading it. He often daydreamed about what he would do if he had some kind of super power. He would fight bad men, of course. Catch all the thieves and the robbers. And if his mother were in danger, he would rescue her! Fly in and POW! He'd beat up the *goondas* and fly off with her!

He smiled at the picture of himself in the role of her saviour. Ma would be so pleased with him! She would be so proud!

Bashonti was having her lunch when he went into the kitchen to dump the ice cream bowl into the basin. She sat on a little red stool and ate while holding on to her plate tightly with her left hand, as though it would slip away from her if she didn't. She looked at Charu and said, "There you are. I thought you had gone to the park."

"We are going to pick up Papa from the airport."

"I know that. So I suppose you won't be asked to go out and play today."

Charu considered this for a few moments. Bashonti Mashi was smiling obliquely at him. He noticed suddenly how prominent the black hairs on her upper lip were. She was like a cat, he thought. A big, fat cat with whiskers. Then he spun around and left the kitchen, making his way to the living room where Ma was chatting with Nikhil. Behind them, the butter yellow curtains billowed softly now and then, stirred by the cool air blowing in from outside. The room was shaded and tranquil. Charu heard his mother laugh and the sound tinkled around him like giddy musical notes. How pretty Ma looked when she laughed, Charu thought happily. She wore a red sleeveless top and a long blue skirt. Her calves seemed like slivers of moonlight when she crossed and uncrossed her legs and her pink toenails were bright as flower petals. Why, Ma was more beautiful than Deepika Padukone, Charu thought wonderingly, looking at his mother's laughing, brilliant eyes. He had anointed Deepika Padukone the most beautiful woman in the world after watching

Bajirao Mastani on television recently. But no, his mother was definitely much more pretty.

"We'll leave in an hour, Charu," Nikhil said to him.

"Okay. Shall I go to the park for a bit then," he asked Nandini.

"All right. But wear your watch. And come back at 3.45 sharp."

Charu strapped on his Mickey Mouse watch, laced up his sneakers and went out, gently shutting the door behind him. In the park the cricket match was in progress already.

"Charooo, you want to fee-ld?" The boy who was bowling called out to him.

"No, I'm going out soo–oon," Charu shouted back.

He strolled around the walking track that skirted the park. The ground was squelchy with fallen leaves–yellow and brown and sodden. There were flowers too, some late laburnum and those small yellow bell-like flowers that he loved so much. They had blazed wildly in the summer sun and now lay mutilated by the first monsoon shower.

Charu adored the park. He came here every afternoon. On holidays, he came in the mornings too. The early mornings were the best. You could see masses of squirrels scampering about then. They skittered away if you came near, twitching up their *jharoo* tails as they ran away. But if you sat quietly on a bench, they didn't mind you and went about their work. He could spend hours watching their minute gleaming eyes, their grey-brown striped fur, and their ceaseless gathering and clambering.

Bashonti's words came back to him now. She had said something about Ma and Nikhil sending him out to play. Why did she say it? He came here every evening anyway. The only time he didn't feel like going to the park to play was when Nikhil came over on Saturdays or Sundays. He wanted to hang out with him because Nikhil was his friend too. And then Ma might say,

"Charu, aren't you going out to play today? Your friends will miss you, won't they?"

Some days that made him go off. But he didn't go because Bunny, Rakesh or Parnika were waiting for him to join them. He went because the park missed him. This patch of wild fenced off by the thicket of apartment blocks all around murmured up to him. And Charu ran out to meet it.

So what was Bashonti Mashi talking about, he puzzled. Her words had set off uneasy ripples in his mind. They lapped at the edges of his consciousness and he felt their meaning hovering close, as if he would grasp it if he thought about it some more. But then he shied away from it like he would from an arithmetic sum he might come back to later.

There was a whoop of laughter and Charu turned and saw that Dimpy had slipped in the slush and fallen down. He soon scrambled to his feet, looking tearful as he did so, and everyone laughed, pointing at his blue bermudas and yellow shirt all brown with mud. The boy's mother, who had evidently been watching, shouted from her balcony, "Dimpy! I told you not to go into the *keechad*! Come back inside at once!"

That made everyone button up their laughter, though you could tell they were dying to go on laughing at Dimpy and also his bossy mother who ticked him off all the time. Charu giggled too—because Dimpy was such a cry baby and a scaredy cat, because he was already walking off, morosely dragging his cricket bat after him.

Charu checked his watch and seeing that there was time, went and looked up the hibiscus sapling he and his mother had planted at the edge of the park some months ago. "Hello, hibiscus," he said to it. The plant was growing nicely now, sending out tough young shoots and leaves. He couldn't wait for the flowers to come out. They would be big and red and beautiful, he thought, and oh, what fun that would be!

But he knew flowers didn't last long in this park. They got picked as soon as they blossomed. When morning came, the pickers went around sniffing for fresh blooms and yanking them off their stems. The greediest of them all was a woman in a dirty white saree who crept into the park early in the morning and plucked loads of those yellow bell-shaped flowers. She stood on a bench under the low hanging branches of the tree and picked them until she had filled up her small plastic bag. The first time he spotted her, Charu had been mad with rage. He ran up to her and and asked her shakily why she was taking the flowers away. She looked down at him once. Then she continued raiding the tree, balancing herself carefully on the arm of the bench, her grimy heels mocking Charu silently.

Angry tears sprang into his eyes. "You're not to take them!" he told her, raising his voice into a futile, tinny scream. The woman ignored him. Hot with humiliation, he ran back into the house. "Ma, why is that woman plucking the yellow flowers," he asked Nandini, panting slightly. "They are so pretty! Why is she taking them away? Make her stop!"

Nandini knelt and hugged him. "Don't be upset, Babu," she cooed at him. "This is a public park. You and I know we should not pick flowers and spoil something beautiful. But there are some people who don't understand this. They have no sense. How do you reason with vandals?"

"What is a vandals," Charu asked, momentarily distracted and slightly pacified.

"Vandal–plural vandals," said Nandini and explained the meaning to him.

"Vandal," Charu repeated and squirrelled the word away.

A little after 4 pm, they set off for the airport in Nikhil's silver grey Innova. Charu climbed into the back seat and fastened the seat belt as he had been taught to. The belt was too broad for his small torso. But the press of it on his chest was reassuring. He felt snug and safe strapped to the car, this car in which his mother and Nikhil were taking him. The seat in front hid Nandini from his view. He could only see the nimbus of her wavy hair and a part of her face when she looked sideways to speak to Nikhil.

He found two packets of Lays chips in the seat flap. He tore one open with his teeth and said, "Ma, you want? Nikhil, you want some?"

"Nope, you go ahead, buddy," Nikhil said. And Nandini turned around and smiled, "No, thank you, Charu. Nikhil, you're such a bad influence! Keeping chips in the car," she said in that pretend-cross voice of hers.

Charu looked out the window contentedly. They sped along the Ring Road, crossing flyover after flyover. There was no water-logging to be seen anywhere, but the sky had become overcast once again. And soon, a soft, whispering rain began to fall.

Nandini let out a groan. "Oh no, it's raining again."

"Relax, it's just a drizzle," said Nikhil.

"I don't know why Ananth ALWAYS picks this peak rush hour to land in Delhi. It's such a bad time! I know it's Saturday, but even then! It's really the worst time of the day! And if this rain doesn't stop we'll get stuck in a jam."

"Relax. *Main hoon na*," Nikhil said, his voice liquid with laughter.

By the time they got to the airport, the rain was falling hard. Nandini called Ananth.

"Papa has just landed," she said to Charu, twisting around to look at him.

Then she said anxiously, "Oh god, Ananth will get totally drenched by the time he gets into the car."

Nikhil made a slightly irritated sound.

"Hey, it won't kill him, okay? I'd take the car closer if I could. But you know I can't."

Nandini sounded annoyed as well. "Nikhil, I wasn't *asking* you to take the car closer!"

They drove into the pick-up lane. Ananth appeared, wheeling a suitcase. He was tall and well-built and smartly dressed in beige trousers and a maroon shirt that were now darkly wet in the rain. Water streamed down his face and the hair on his forearms lay slick and flat. Nikhil got out and they thumped each other on the back briefly. Then they opened the rear hatch, put in the suitcase and quickly got into the car. On any other day Nandini would have switched seats and let Ananth sit in the front, but thanks to the pounding rain, she remained where she was.

"God, this effing rain," Ananth said, rubbing his head with a small towel that Nikhil had produced from somewhere.

"Ananth!" Nandini said reproachfully.

"Hey, Babe! "Yeah, yeah, I know. I'm out of practice child-proofing my vocab. But I didn't actually use the word, did I?" Then he turned to Charu who was trying to figure out what 'effing' meant.

"So how's the little big guy doing," Ananth said to Charu, making a clown face.

Charu gave him a shy smile.

"I got you something."

"What?"

"Wait till we get home!"

They drove out of the airport and joined a stream of traffic that was already beginning to sputter and choke. The wipers swished rhythmically on the windscreen, drawing swift arcs of clarity which the rain obscured at once. It had become murky outside, the afternoon transiting directly into evening without stopping for a breath of twilight. The street lights glowed wanly through the rain, looking on like giant yellow eyeballs. Nikhil nosed the Innova into a phalanx of cars which were all turning right. Soon they were part of a mass of vehicles that stood like petrified cattle under the violent rain. They remained frozen in that attitude for a long, long time. The jam that they had been dreading the whole day was finally upon them—ballooning, immense, radiating out in ever widening circles and shooting its tendrils up every street and alleyway to bind and gag the city.

An hour later, they had progressed no more than a few of kilometres since leaving the airport. The rain had slackened off, but not the traffic snarl it had spawned. The cars were back to back, inches away from each other, imprisoned in their collective urban misery. The air smelt of warm rain and gritty exhaust, and the poisonous taste of metal clung to their tongues. With its AC switched off, the car felt crowded and sweaty. Stop. Go. Stop. Go. Stop. It was as if they were caught in an eternal loop of lurching and halting as they made their excruciating crawl up the rise of a never-ending flyover.

Charu fidgeted in his seat. He had finished the second packet of chips long ago. He was thirsty now but he dared not have a gulp of water from the bottle that Nikhil kept in the car. He needed to pee and the water would only make things worse, he knew.

And here was the jam closing in from all sides. He remembered that scene in *Jurassic Park* where the boy and the girl were trapped inside the overturned car. The T-Rex was shaking it and flattening it like a toy. Suddenly, he felt their terror.

"I need to go to the loo, Ma", he said softly.

"So do I," Nikhil said ruefully. "Come on, Charu, hold it. You can do it, buddy. After a while the pee dries up inside."

"Ha ha, that's funny," said Ananth.

He had been checking their route on Google Maps every few minutes. "Oh, boy, we've been stuck in Munirka for the last half an hour. And it's a thick red line all the way to GK 2," he said. "It says here this will take another hour and fifty minutes! Why is there a jam anyway? I didn't see any water-logging!"

"Probably heavy water-logging further down. GK, Lajpat Nagar...they have a cascading effect," said Nikhil. "Well, we just have to grin and bear it," he shrugged. "Who wants to listen to some music?"

"Please!" Nandini said sharply. "I'm in no mood to listen to music. Ananth, I don't know WHY you have to pick this time of the day to land in Delhi," she said. "Every time! Without fail!"

"I think you've made that point already, Nandini," Ananth said. "Probably thrice in the last one hour. Rain like this and you know Delhi will choke up at any time of the day."

"I did make the point, as I have made it on other occasions. But I wonder if you even listened. Or paid attention. I didn't hear you say that you made a mistake!"

"Guys, we are stuck in a jam. We could be here for hours. Would help if you quit scrapping," Nikhil said.

"I'm not scrapping," Nandini said in a low voice. She didn't turn her head towards Ananth when she spoke, but looked straight ahead. Her flyaway hair glowed red-brown in the wash of the yellow street lights. "I'm done scrapping with Ananth."

"What's that supposed to mean," Ananth snapped.

"It means that I'm done getting agitated about the way you carry on without thinking about others!"

"Hello! Am I hearing you right? Why the fuck am I sweating my guts out in that godforsaken place in the boondocks of Andhra? Shall I quit and come away? Maybe you can support us all on the pittance you earn?"

"Guys, guys..." Nikhil said. But neither of them paid any attention to his feeble interjection. They pitched headlong into their row, Nandini smouldering up ahead, and Ananth, resentful that he was at the back, at a situational disadvantage vis-a-vis his wife, but determined to slash and burn just the same.

"First off," hissed Nandini. "I've told you not to swear in front of the child. Second, we both know why you accepted this assignment. You were promised a promotion after your stint there. You could have said no. Other opportunities would have come. You had a choice. You could have chosen not to shirk your responsibilities and leave. You didn't do it for us. You did it in spite of us. You did it for your own goddamn self!"

"Are you finished with your lecture? We've had this conversation before. I did not have a choice. I could not pass it up. And if you were so keen to keep the family together, why the fuck didn't you accompany me? Wives do. Not as if you're earning a six-figure salary here! You just need an excuse to start yammering and complaining! God, you're such a crashing bore, Nandini! Even your arguments are boring!"

"Hey, take it easy, *yaar.* Watch what you're saying," Nikhil said angrily. "And Nandini, you shut up too, okay! You guys have no sense?"

Charu could hear his mother beginning to cry. He felt hot stinging tears well up in his own eyes too. He had pushed himself against the door of the car, as far away from his father as possible. He was sick with claustrophobia. The Innova seemed to have shrunk in size, squeezed and crushed by the monster jam all around. How long would they be here, he thought desperately. The pressure on his bladder was unbearable now. And there was a painful squeezing in his throat as he watched his mother crying into her hands, her head bowed, her red-brown hair waterfalling down.

"Nandini, please," Nikhil said with a catch in his voice. He extended an arm to comfort her. At which Nandini cried a little more.

Ananth said pleasantly, "Hey, Nicks, I shall console my wife in good time, all right? You can quit lending your sympathetic shoulder."

Nikhil threw up his hands.

"Oh, this is just great," he exclaimed.

"Ma, I need to go," Charu said loudly.

"Just a little bit longer, Babu," Nandini turned around and said in a wet, muffled voice. Her face looked leaky, as if it were disintegrating. But she slipped into her soothing, mothery tone. "Can't you hold on for just a bit more?"

It was nearly nine when they finally reached home. Nikhil hauled out the suitcase, muttered a casual "See you around" to no one in particular, and then drove away.

They showered and changed and sat down to dinner. Bashonti served them. Ananth ribbed her and said she had put on more weight. Bashonti grinned and preened.

"Charu, please finish your food," Nandini said, as if it were business as usual, as if it were just another mealtime. Charu glanced at her. She was wearing a pair of loose shorts and a faded grey T-shirt with I Love Paris emblazoned on it. Her slim gold bangle clinked against the table as she moved her hand. The journey back home had been horrid. He wished he had not gone with them. But Ma looked calm. It seemed as though she had scrubbed the evening off herself. And his father was wolfing down the chicken curry and rice in a perfectly normal way.

"Babu doesn't eat enough," Bashonti said, addressing herself to Ananth. "You should take him to a doctor."

"He needs more exercise," Ananth said, speaking with his mouth full of chicken curry and rice.

Charu was dreaming of that woman in the half-dirty saree who came to pick flowers. Only this time there were others with her. She was leading an army of people who had come to strip the park of its flowers. They went from tree to tree, tearing out the blooms. Yellow, red, pink, violet–the flowers were falling to the ground with a soft, dying plop. They worked quickly, efficiently, plucking them like eyes out of a face until every plant and tree in the park was eyeless and unseeing. Then they took out their sharp saws and began to hack at the trees. Charu wanted to shout and tell them to stop. But he found that he had lost his voice. The trees were falling now. Crack! Snap! Crash!

The sounds rent his dream and he woke up.

He rubbed his eyes and whimpered a little. He wanted his mother. He got up and went towards her bedroom, almost in a trance, impelled by the fear of things unknown. Standing outside her door he could hear noises inside. That's when he remembered that his father was here. He turned the handle and opened the door.

The room was in semi-darkness, lit only by a shaft of light that came from the bathroom and lay upon the floor like the blade of a sword. Charu discerned two figures on the bed. It took him a few seconds to realise that Nandini was lying spreadeagled with her arms stretched over her head. Ananth held down her arms with his big hands and had her pinioned with his naked body. "No!" Nandini cried through her clenched teeth. Her T-shirt was bunched around her waist and her pale stricken legs looked like the severed branches from his dream.

"Please, no," his mother cried out again.

"Bitch," his father spat out and slammed into her.

Charu let go the door and came back to his room. He climbed into his bed and curled himself up, burrowing his head into his knees, fisting his hands and tightly shutting his eyes. "Vandal, vandal, vandal," he whispered into the darkness that was pouring into his mind and slowly rocked himself to sleep.

Acknowledgements

I would like to thank Niyogi Books for publishing this book, and my editor Mohua Mitra for editing it with such insight and sensitivity. I am grateful to Nirmal Kanti Bhattacharjee, Tultul Niyogi and Bikash Niyogi, without whose encouragement and support this book would not have been possible.

Most of these stories were written after I moved to Delhi in 2014. A big thank you to friends Parul Chandra, Prasanto K. Roy and Mahasweta Ghosh Roy, who helped me find my way in a new city and made my Delhi experience rewarding.

I am grateful to my husband Sanjay; my late father, who was the true rock of my life; and last, but not the least, I would like to thank my mother for instilling in me the love of literature and for believing in me always.

Shuma Raha can be reached on Twitter @ShumaRaha